NEUMONAH

NEUMONAH

and the Chantallah

S.J. ZERCHER

Chantallah

Also by S.J. Zercher

Monahdah (Book 1)

My Magic

"You will hear of a dwelling place in the heavens, above the earth, that shall fall with a great crash. It will appear as a blue star. Very soon after this, the ceremonies of my people will cease."—White Feather

Two young Hopi brothers walk through the desert, hunting for snakes. The Arizona sun beats down, leaving cracks in the mud puddles from the previous storm. It's October 16th, and the hottest day on record. The younger brother carries an empty black sack, and the older one carries a long stick. Ten yards ahead of them, snagged in some sagebrush, lies a bright, red winter hat. Simultaneously, they reach the hat.

Chuchip pulls on the hat. "Let go!"

Hania looks up at his big brother and tries to stand taller than he is. "I saw it first."

"I'm older. You should give it to me," says Chuchip.

Hania gives in, drops the hat, and walks away. "Asshole," he says under his breath.

Chuchip watches him walk away. "But since I'm nicer, I'll let you have it." He pushes it down over his brother's eyes.

"Cut it out, Chip!"

"Apologize for calling me an asshole!"

"Alright, geez...sorry." Hania adjusts the hat over his long, silky black hair.

"Listen!" Chuchip points. The sound of a rattlesnake in a bush next to them interrupts.

"He's mad, thanks to you," says Hania backing away.

Chuchip removes his snake wand from his back pocket, a stick with two feathers on the end. Hania holds back the branches of the bush with the long staff. Coiled up between two rocks, and camouflaged perfectly, the snake rattles his tail on high alert. "I see him. He's right there. Get him away from those rocks."

Hania uses the staff to guide the snake out of the bush. The rattlesnake gets ready to strike. "Grab him," yells Hania. The snake targets Hania, but Hania quickly dodges the venomous strike and turns away. "Forget this one. He's too mad."

"You want Moki to win again? Hold him down with the staff."

Hania pins the snake to the ground in the groove at the end of the staff, suited just for this purpose. Chuchip soothes the snake with his feather wand, brushing it along its diamond-back scales. "That's it. Watch me do my magic." The snake stops his rattle, and Chuchip carefully grabs the snake from behind the head and picks him up. "Get the sack," he whispers.

Hania runs to the place where he dropped the sack. Chuchip says something in Hopi, and Hania stops running and slowly walks over. His brother gently puts the docile snake in the black sack and ties a knot.

A blue ball flashes across the sky. Hania shields his eyes from the brightness. "What was that?"

"A meteor entering the atmosphere, I think. They look like fireballs."

With a full sack of snakes, they return to the village.

Moki walks over to Chuchip for a fist bump. "Five bro," he says with a big grin. "Who's the boss?"

"Not you," says Chuchip. "We have one more than you. Navay."

"Shit." Moki gives his sack to the snake priest, Chuchip and Hania's father.

"Watch your mouth." The snake priest dips a snake into a large glass jar of water and herbs. After cleansing each snake in this manner, he tosses them into a bed of sand. A snake tries to leave the sand circle, but Chuchip uses the staff and prevents him from escaping.

The blazing Arizona sun sets, and with quiet anticipation, the Snake clans fast in their kivas while the snakes await.

Snake Dance

The main plaza flows with people from the first, second, and third mesas. Many wear traditional ceremonial clothing, red cloth headdresses, airy cotton pants wrapped by ornate belts of silver and turquoise, deerskin moccasins, and painted faces.

Soft, morning light shines on the black painted faces in the Kivas, and eyes glow in the darkness. After a night of prayer and meditation below, the priests climb the ladder to the world above. One by one, they circle the plaza, stepping in unison to the beat of their rattles. They sprinkle sacred corn meal onto the snake shrine with each passing. Feather head-dresses sway from side to side—step, shake, step, shake. After several passes, they separate and form two lines.

The slithering snakes are released from the shrine. A priest puts a snake in his mouth. The snake hangs down on either side of his face and body. He continues the dance around the plaza. Women in black shawls throw corn meal on the snake priest.

When the prayers for a healthy harvest reach the snakes, the priest tosses them to the side, while the snake gatherer picks them up and follows behind the priest. He soothes the snakes with a feather wand. This doesn't prevent venomous snake bites, however. Blood drips down his neck, arms, and legs.

Drums continue—boom, boom, boom—and the rattles hold the spirit of the people. Young children marvel at the snake gatherers. Hania weaves through the crowd, making his way to the front to stand next to his brother. Thirty smooth, limp snakes drape across the snake gatherer's arms and one coils around his neck. It's hard to see where one snake begins and another one ends.

Their father creates a large circle of meal on the plaza floor. The gatherers release all the snakes into the circle, and the girls of the snake clan throw meal on the huge, slithering pile. Four priests, including the boys' father, gather them up and run out of the plaza. With armfuls of snakes, they run to one of the four sacred directions.

Chuchip's father motions to him for help. Hania wants to help too, but his father only needs Chuchip. Happily, Chuchip gathers up two snakes and runs behind his father to the special shrine where they release the snakes. From the shrine, the snakes carry out their prayers.

Hania walks away, scuffing his feet in the dirt, disappointed, and wanders away into the desert in a pout. He goes to his favorite rock where he likes to sit whenever he feels troubled.

After drinking an emetic to induce nausea, Chuchip's father vomits, purging himself of any snake magic. All the other priests are doing the same, signaling the end to the ceremony.

Hania comes running back into the plaza with a bothered look on his face, and his mother calls for him.

"Why has the color left your face?" she says in Hopi.

"There's someone here. A visitor."

"We're not open today to the public," she says.

"That's what I told him, and he wouldn't leave. He gave me this." He puts a stone tablet with strange markings in her hand.

"Where did you get this?" Her harsh tone makes him nervous.

"I told you. This weird guy," he says partly in English. She darts away with the tablet.

He runs after her. "Wait! What about the guy? He's over by the rocks."

His mother finds her father who's enjoying the late afternoon sun radiating off the adobe wall. He sits in a folding chair against one of the homes in the village, conversing with her brother.

When Grandfather has something to say, which is not very often, everyone stops and listens. That's why the sudden interruption from Hania's mother is taken by surprise. She hands Grandfather the stone tablet with the strange carvings. Grandfather only speaks in their native dialect and will only answer to those who do the same.

"Hania has this." Her hand trembles.

"I didn't take it. It's from this man—a foreigner."

"You are the keeper for the sacred tablets. You should put it where it belongs." She scolds.

Hania's uncle takes the tablet and looks closely at the inscription. He stirs out of his afternoon slumber. "Explain this, Hania."

"Someone gave it to me."

Hania looks at his mom as she glares at him. Grandfather walks away with the stone tablet. "I didn't take it. Where is Grandfather going?"

"To put it back... where it belongs."

"Why don't you believe me?"

Uncle leaves the comfort of the chair and follows Grandfather. "Now where are you going?" Mother says crossly to her brother.

"To see."

They follow Grandfather into his house. He leaves the room, pulls back a rug, and removes a wooden box from the floor. He returns with a small bundle and sets it down on the table. He opens the blanket revealing three tablets, just like the one Hania gave him.

Uncle scratches his chin. "All the stones are here. Where did this stone come from?"

"I told you. A man gave it to me. He's at the rocks." Hania feels the gravity of the situation.

Grandfather's eyes are old but bright. He looks straight into Hania's eyes. "What did he say, this man?" Everyone turns and looks at Hania.

"He asked me, 'Who is your creator?' 'What clan belonged my mother?' Then he said, 'We are brothers' and gave me the stone tablet."

"It could be a replica," Uncle says with apprehension.

"He instructed me to tell you... he made it sound like a matter of life or death, to find him in the morning at first light."

"He speaks English?" asks Grandfather.

"I don't know. He said this in Hopi, but he is Anglo and very tall. He wears strange clothes."

"Could it be?" Hania's mother's eyes open wide. "Pahana?"

Grandfather puts a hand on Hania's shoulder. "You did well, Hania. At first light, we shall go see what this person is about."

Like a Suspect

Beverly empties a bucket and rings out a wash rag in the

muck sink in a utility room. At a booth, she takes off a shoe and massages the bottom of her foot.

The restaurant phone rings. "Hello?" she answers. "Hi, Bean." She puts her shoe back on. "You're welcome. I didn't mind." Beverly rubs her back. "No. Not yet. I'll let you know if I hear from her." She looks at the door. "He's on his way over now? Okay, Bean. Feel better."

A police officer walks through the door holding something.

"Hey, Billy. We just closed, but I can get you one last cup of coffee."

"Oh, that's okay. Bean wanted me to give you this casserole."

"Oh. She didn't have to do that."

"She appreciates you working her shift and knows you've been worried about Anah. I also wanted to ask you some questions."

"I told you everything I know."

"We have a witness who saw Anah leave the Coffee House in Albuquerque pretty upset."

"A witness?"

"Someone in her class." He removes his hat and sets it on the counter.

"Did this person know where she was going?"

"No."

Beverly sits at the booth. "What did you want to ask me?"

"The names of people she might've hung out with. Do you know of anyone at school or around town?"

"She usually came home on the weekends, you know.

Sometimes she'd hang out with her friends from high school. She hadn't met anyone that I know of, yet, at the university."

"Did your daughter ever mention her friend, Alan?"

"Never heard of him." Beverly yawns.

Billy puts his hat back on. "Okay. Thanks, Beverly. Go home and get some rest. You look beat."

Beverly locks the door behind him, turns the sign from open to closed, and sits down at a booth. She lays on her back. She dozes off. A knock at the door startles her.

She points to the sign. "We're closed."

A young man, wearing black framed glasses and an old brown tweed jacket, looks at Beverly through the glass door and knocks again.

Beverly speaks through the closed door. "I'm sorry we're not open."

"I'm looking for Anah's Mom."

"And you are?"

He pushes his glasses up the bridge of his nose. "I'm her friend from school."

Beverly opens the door a crack.

"I'm looking for Anah Rice. I was told her mother works here. Do you know where I can find her?"

Beverly cautiously opens the door. "What's your name?"

"Oh... sorry. My name's Alan."

"I'm Beverly. Anah's Mom. You two are friends?"

"We just met, actually, in physics class...you know, it's only our first semester."

"Would you like some coffee?"

"Sure. Thanks."

"The last cup is always the best." Beverly empties the last of the coffee into a couple of mugs.

"The police have questioned me, twice now. Anah's disappearance has been, well, strange. It's very unnerving."

Beverly has a sip. "If you've done nothing wrong, then don't worry about it."

"I was the last person to see her, besides her cousin. What's his name?"

"Yemo."

"I want you to know that, for what it's worth, after the Coffee House, I have no idea what happened."

Beverly perks up and leans closer. "What did you tell the police?"

Alan pushes his glasses up. "Anah asked me to hang out with her at the Coffee House. At first, I said no, because, well, I thought her cousin was her boyfriend, and he acted weird around her—like he was her bodyguard or something. So, we went there, and it was packed, you know, full of college kids, mostly. I didn't think we'd get a table, but we did, which was weird..."

"Weird how?"

"Well, I'm pretty sure Anah knew what table to get before it became available."

"Were they getting their stuff to leave?" Beverly knows exactly what he's referring to. This is one of Anah's "tricks". She has no tolerance for long lines.

"They were drinking coffee and looking at their computers...absolutely no indication they were leaving. Anyway, we got a table, and Yemo was there talking to students about football and ice hockey...also weird." Alan makes a face at the memory.

"What's so weird about football or ice hockey?"

"He wanted to try ice hockey. Said it looked interesting to maneuver around on those—'shoes'. He didn't know what they were called, like everything's new to him, like he's from another planet. It's also peculiar how the school has no record of him. He attended classes, lived in a dorm, and yet the school has no idea who he was. The teachers claim to not remember him either, which, I guess, could happen in a class size of 80 students, but he didn't go unnoticed. Teachers either loved him or hated him. He always had something to say, most of which was to correct the teacher. Everyone knew him, and no one seems to remember him!"

"You do."

"Obviously." He removes his glasses to rub his eyes before putting them back on. "I feel like I'm going crazy."

"Did you tell the police about him?" Beverly taps her finger on her coffee mug.

He shakes his head. "I don't know why I didn't. I meant to, but then it left my mind. When I did remember, I had this strong impulse to not mention him. A voice told me that I couldn't. Then I decided to find you."

"To conduct your own investigation?"

"Yeah, I guess."

Beverly's eyes narrow. "Then what? Is that all?"

"Oh, uhh... this is the part that keeps running around in my head," he continues. "Yemo says something about how we should converse like humans or not at all, just out of the blue, and he looks really disturbed like he's the Terminator. The guy's weird, right? Then he tells Anah to stay put as he gets up and follows someone, a huge dude, some modern day viking, out of the coffee house."

"Anah stayed with you at the coffee house?"

"Well, no. She got up. Said she would be back and followed Yemo across the street. I watched her through the window. The traffic light turned from green to red, and I haven't seen her since."

"Is the light not supposed to turn from green to red?"

"It's green, yellow, then red. It can turn from red to green, but not the other way around."

Beverly takes a sip of coffee and says, "I'm not sure what you're getting at."

"I saw the whole thing. The light just turned green, then it suddenly turned red, causing traffic to a screeching halt." He takes a breath and a sip of his coffee.

"That's everything you remember?"

He pauses, reaches into his pocket, and places a cell phone on the table. "This is Anah's. She left it on the table at the coffee house."

"The police didn't take the phone?"

Alan picks up the phone and goes to the pictures. "I kept it to myself. I was able to hack the phone. Anah sent you this picture." Beverly looks at the picture of Anah and Yemo.

"It says, 'Happy Birthday! See you tomorrow, with love, your favorite 'twins.'"

"It was my birthday, the day before they disappeared."

"I think you're missing the point. It says 'twins'. Anah told me that Yemo is her cousin."

"Right, well, that's an inside joke. I always tease them about how much they act and look alike. You know, more like siblings than cousins."

"I checked her calls. Ten days up to the day she disappeared are on here. Nothing unusual, except one thing. She has no number programmed in for her twin/cousin."

"What's weird about that?"

"You don't think that's weird? They were always together, but they had no way to call or text if needed. You know, to say, 'Hey, where are you, or I'm gonna be late.'"

"Look, Alan, you're thinking way too hard about this. Yemo doesn't have a phone."

"I just thought you might want to know what happened to Anah."

"Of course, I do. She's my daughter."

"If there's something you're not telling me..."

Beverly sets her coffee mug down. "What business is it of yours?"

"I'm sorry. It's just...I'm not sleeping...staying awake thinking about all this. I feel like I'm going crazy. It's messed up, and I think Yemo is behind it somehow."

"How do you think I feel?"

He looks into his coffee mug. "Why would Yemo say to

talk like a human or not at all? What do you think he meant by that?"

"He was being funny."

"He wasn't joking. This was right before he tailed that dude, and we haven't seen them since."

"I really must get back to work, Alan. I appreciate your visit. When I hear from Anah, I'll be sure to let you know."

"Sure," Alan says, adjusting his eyeglasses. "Thank you for letting me talk this through with you. I'm sorry for sounding like a jerk. I can't imagine how you must feel." He grabs a pen and a notepad out from his inside pocket. "Here's my number. Could you ask her to call me if you do?"

"Okay, Alan. It was nice to meet you. I'm sorry it's under these circumstances."

"Me, too."

She locks the door behind him and returns to the booth. She looks at the picture of Anah and Yemo on the cell phone. "No word...no goodbye. They must have been in danger."

Nakwach

"When the star people come, we won't know if they'll be for us or against us"—Native Elder

I

t's an unusually dark, quiet morning. Bright, crisp stars flicker above the village of Hotevilla. Everyone lies awake and silent in their beds. This is the morning they will remember before everything changes. History and Legend have merged, and this life will be behind them. They have come face to face with prophecy.

Not a single hair is out of place. His thick, silver bangs frame his wise, stern face. Grandfather buttons up his shirt. The one he wears for only special occasions, like when he was a guest at the White House.

Hania's mother shakes him out of his slumber. "Wake now, Hania," she says.

Hania will take them to the spot where he spoke with the visitor. He puts on his black Levis, his black hoody, and his sneakers. The air is cold, and he sees his breath.

The eastern horizon is burnt orange and pale blue. Many families have already gathered in front of Grandfather's house. Hania retraces his steps from the previous day. Perhaps he would still be lying in his warm bed, had he not behaved so childishly.

"Do you know where exactly?" asks his mother.

Hania rubs the sleep out of his eyes. "He said at the rock."

"That could be anywhere," she says.

A cool morning breeze sharpens his memory. "This way," he points. "I was over here."

They arrive at a large overhang and wait for what seems like an eternity. Except for a few birds flying across the sky, all is still. Sirius, the brightest star in the sky, flickers over the southern mountains. Without turning away or blinking an eye, they stare to the East and welcome the sunrise. They want to hold this sunrise in their memory forever, for this may be their last. Collectively, they put aside their past grievances with one another and embrace the moment with open hearts. They integrate with Spirit, on that overhang, and become one as a nation of people. They are the Earth, the sky, the sun, and the moon. This is a day of redemption, a day of reckoning, and a day of prophecy. Prayer can no longer save them. Only past deeds and how that translates in the eyes of Pahana.

A tall silhouette appears against the crimson sky. He stands about eight feet tall. His body is well-defined, underneath a blue, iridescent suit. On the front of his suit is an insignia of interlocking triangles. His dark, hazel eyes are large, almost too large, but warm and kind. His black boots fit close to the foot, like an extra layer of skin.

Grandfather instructs everyone not to speak. He has reservations and will not be made a fool. Apprehensively, he approaches the strange man, in the funny, blue suit, and holds out his arm with his palm facing up. If the visitor really is the true white brother, he will understand. The stranger smiles and steps closer, accepting the test. He places his palm on top of Grandfather's and they clasp. Hania knows this is the nakwach, an ancient symbol of brotherhood. Grandfather cries tears of joy and sorrow. He questions the reality of the moment because it has always been this way in his dreams. The others gather around Grandfather and the visitor, placing hand on top of hand. They walk to the village and sit at the home of Hania's and Chuchip's mother and father. Grandfather speaks with the visitor for almost an hour, further confirming the identity of the man. Hania listens and struggles to understand. He wishes he tried harder to speak his mother tongue.

Hania stands next to his brother and looks up at him. "Chip, what are they saying?"

Chuchip walks to his room and sits on his bed. Hania sits next to him. "This is real." Chuchip removes his hoodie. "That guy—he's a freakin' alien. His dialect is hard to understand."

"Do you?" Hania wraps his arms around his knees.

Chip gets up and stares out the window. "He's here to help us. There's some kind of galactic war, and a lot of people are going to die."

"What did the nakwach mean?" asks Hania.

"It's like they had some kind of agreement or arrangement, and he's here to honor it."

"What agreement?"

"Stop asking questions."

"You think I'm too young or too stupid."

"Don't be stupid!"

"See!"

"I have to listen, so be quiet."

Chuchip listens to the Hopi dialect the visitor speaks, hoping his ear will recognize some meaning. Grandfather stays quiet, listening. His questions reveal context. He asks about living conditions—if they will be forced to live on a new reservation, and if he and the elders are too old to survive the trip.

"What are they saying?" Hania hisses.

"That they, whoever they are, will take us somewhere."

"I've never been out of Arizona."

"Hania, it would be like, not even on this planet, because the whole planet is..."

"Is what?"

Fear grows inside Hania, like thick goo.

"Hey." He nudges him. "Don't worry, brother," he speaks in Hopi. "I won't let anyone force us to do anything we don't want to do."

Navajo Trail

Alan pulls over to look at his phone for directions. He has no cell service, and his fuel gauge is in the red. He's kicking himself for not buying a map like his father advised him. "You shouldn't solely rely on technology," he can hear his father scold.

Alan's been driving on the Navajo Trail for what seems like forever and hasn't seen anything but dust devils and a quick lizard crossing the road. He makes a U-turn and goes back toward a small town he passed 45 minutes ago. The sun will set in a few hours, and he'd rather drive the rest of the way at daybreak. Plus, he needs a map.

Exploring the West was the main reason he chose the University of New Mexico. He looked forward to Fall break and hiking in The Grand Canyon. Anah would have come along, he thinks, had he a chance to ask before she disappeared.

His Subaru putters and runs out of gas. He pulls off the side of the road and comes to a stop. He walks the last 200 yards to the gas station, buys a gas can, fills it, and walks back to his car. The late afternoon sun beats down on him. He stops to take a drink from his water bottle.

A coyote sits next to an old white sign that reads, Coal Mine Campground 2.5 miles. While filling his tank, Alan stares back at the coyote. "What are you looking at?" It runs into the desert as if he suddenly remembered something.

The car starts, to Alan's relief, and he drives the rest of the way into town and parks in front of the hotel. The lobby is hot and stuffy. Alan approaches the front desk. "Hi, I would like a room please."

"Just you?" The woman behind the desk wears bright pink barrettes, one on each side of her head.

"Yes." Alan removes his glasses and wipes his perspiration. "It's really hot in here."

"My apologies. Air conditioner is getting repaired. How many nights?"

"Just for tonight. I'm on my way to the Grand Canyon. Do you know how long it takes to get there from here?"

"You have about three more hours. How would you like to pay for that?"

"How much is the room?"

"With tax, it's 126 dollars and 15 cents."

Alan's parents gave him strict instructions to use the credit card only for gas and emergencies, so he will convince them this is an emergency.

"I'm sorry this card isn't going through," she says.

"Could you try again, please?" Alan looks through his wallet to count his cash. "I don't have enough cash."

"There's a campsite about sixteen miles from here, 'Coal Mine'. Head east, right here, on 264."

"Thanks." He stuffs his credit card into his wallet and leaves the hotel.

Alan checks his phone. Still no signal. "What the hell?" He walks back in and approaches the front desk again. "Is there cell phone service here?"

"Yes."

"I have no signal."

The woman looks at her phone. "Huh... I'm not sure why that is."

"Do you have wifi?"

"Yes," she looks at her computer. "Wait. Actually, no... it seems to be down. That happens, you know, depending on how many people are using it. Also, if you would like to do the tour of the villages it's only 20 bucks and includes lunch. Willy, the guide, could pick you up right at the windmill near the campground at 8:30."

"Okay, thanks."

$$N = R* \cdot fp \cdot Ne \cdot fl \cdot fi \cdot fc \cdot L$$

Alan doesn't waste time getting to the campsite. Watching the sunset over the canyon will make everything right again. He turns down the dusty, dirt road, stops to pay at the drop-off box, and parks next to the old windmill. As the last light dips down into the little canyon, he stands along its edge. A dramatic display of shadows stretches across the canyon floor from the rock pillars. A warm glow on the rocks highlights the variations of colors of orange, red, and white in the sandstone and continues to change in hue as the sun gradually sinks behind the mountains to the West.

Alan reaches into his little red cooler, cracks open a cola, grabs a bag of popcorn, and climbs up onto the roof of his Subaru. The early evening sky transitions into night. A coyote cackles, igniting a chorus of coyotes on the other side of the canyon.

Night settles, and the stars look like bright pinholes in a black canvas. Alan has never seen this many stars. He rests his hands on his stomach and sighs. With wide eyes, he takes in the enormous horizon. A peculiar sensation becomes him. He feels like he's a part of space, traveling in a river of stars at 1.3 million miles per hour. The Milky Way stretches across the sky like a ribbon. In Earth's neighborhood, there are 400 billion stars and just as many planets. According to Drake's Equation, at least 72 intelligent civilizations, in our solar system alone, could exist. This equation gives him comfort and the feeling of not being completely alone in the universe.

As he floats back down to Earth, so do his thoughts. He thinks about Anah. Why did she up and leave like that? Why wasn't her mother a total wreck? Her daughter disappeared! Anah isn't the type to just drop out of school and run away. Something was off.

Movement from the east interrupts his thoughts. Low on the horizon, he sees a formation of bright lights, green and red. He props himself up to get a better look. "What the?" The lights move toward him in a triangular formation. It's difficult to put into perspective how far away, or how close the lights are. They move in unison and slowly move closer. Frozen in awe, he's not sure what he's witnessing. The distance between the lights grows farther apart. Now he understands. The lights belong to a triangular ship, enormous. Hovering now directly above him and completely blocking the view of the sky, he's able to make out different features; lights coming from windows, the ship's smooth, reflective surface, and the size of the craft, at least a mile wide.

Reaching in his coat pocket for his phone, he tries to take a picture. Overcome by the enormous object hovering above him, he falls off the hood of the car, spilling his soda and popcorn on the way down. The back of his head lands on a rock.

At first, Alan doesn't remember a thing. He moans, places his hand on the back of his head, and feels a large lump. Slowly, he sits up and feels around for his glasses. His hand lands on a cactus. Luckily, the glasses are in one piece. He can think and see clearly again. He picks up his cell phone and cola, and after he drinks the last few sips to help quench his terrible thirst, he remembers the ship. Or was it a dream? His head throbs and his mind feels foggy. He climbs into his bedroll in the back of the Subaru. He scrolls through pictures on his phone and is disappointed with the blurry image. It's not a convincing UFO picture, but he saw what he saw.

Star Elders

Morning light shines on Alan's face. He puts on his glasses and rubs the back of his head. The swelling has gone down. He plugs his dead phone into the charger and tries to start the car but the engine won't turn over.

"Crap!" He grabs his backpack, throws in a bottle of water, and walks toward the main road.

A vehicle approaches, and he runs to catch a ride.

"Wait! Stop!" He waves his arms in the air at the van. Alan stands in a cloud of dust. The van stops and turns around. The driver lowers his window. A patch covers his right eye. It's not black, like a pirate, but a design like a Navajo rug that's red, white, and blue.

"Are you doing the tour?"

Alan catches his breath. "Yeah, sure. I'll do the tour."

The door slides open, and Alan climbs in. The smell of sunblock and two older, typical-looking tourists, decked out in khaki hats, khaki pants, and white shirts, greet him. The man has a camera with a big lens around his neck.

"Thanks for turning around. I walked from the campsite."

"Glad I saw you." He adjusts his eyepatch. "I didn't have anyone else on my list," he says apologetically, "otherwise, I would have stopped."

"I didn't sign up. I camped in my car last night, and it wouldn't start this morning... think my battery's dead."

"I can give you a jump on the way back."

"That would be great."

He looks back at Alan from the review mirror. Alan has déja vous. "Hey. Are you Chris Hayes?"

"Ahh...no. People have told me that I look like him. I'm

Alan. I go to the University of New Mexico." Alan removes his glasses and cleans the dust off.

"Nice to meet you, Alan. I'm Willy, your tour guide. This is George and Colleen from Alabama." Alan nods hello. George has his camera in his face taking pictures out the window.

On the drive up to the mesa, Alan wants to ask if anyone saw the huge flying triangle but decides to wait for someone else to mention it first. Willy was talking, anyway, about the history of the villages and the Hopi, so he didn't want to interrupt.

When they reach the village that dates back 1,150 years, Willy points out that the residents have no power or running water.

George stops taking pictures and looks curiously out the window. "Or people."

"180 households live in this village..."

Alan pushes up his glasses and looks around at the desertion. "It looks abandoned."

Everyone looks around at the empty village and streets. A blast of wind picks up a swirl of dust. The adobe and stone buildings are as old as they look. Alan can't believe people live in such bare conditions.

George focuses his camera to take another picture, but Willy puts his hand out. "Please respect our no photography rule for the duration of this tour." Willy knocks on the door of one of the houses. No one answers, so he walks around to the backdoor. He knocks, says something in Hopi, and enters. Alan, and the couple wait outside. George can't help himself and takes another picture. Alan notices the dry corn stalks in the field, looking as sad and lonely as the village.

Alan peeks his head in the doorway. "Is everything okay?"

Willy doesn't answer. He goes to another house and walks right in without knocking. This time, Alan follows inside. Stone tablets are on the table. "What are those?"

Willy stays quiet and raps the tablets in the cloth.

"Willy, where is everyone?"

"Let's go back to the van and head to the next village."

"Is that where everyone is?"

We follow Willy back to the van, and he carries with him the stone tablets. George snaps a picture. "No pictures! Or I'll take your memory card, George."

On the way to the next village, Willy doesn't talk about the Hopi culture. He goes from chatty to mute. When they arrive, it's another ghost town. Willy wanders around the vacant plaza, door to door, in total silence. Alan's curiosity turns eerie. A dog moseys through the plaza, softly whimpering, lost and confused. He looks around at the old buildings of the abandoned village. Everything lies where they left it. The outside ovens are still warm with burnt bread inside.

Willy sits on a bench and Alan sits next to him. "How could a couple of hundred families up and leave without anyone knowing?"

"They came." Willy looks up at the sky with his one eye.

"Who?"

"The star elders."

"Who are they?"

In the distance, a flash of lightning tears through the sky. Alan scuffs up dirt with his white Converse waiting for Willy to answer.

Willy removes a red handkerchief from his jean's back pocket and wipes his neck. "If it means what I think it means, then something is going down."

"Last night at the campground, I saw something." He takes out his phone and shows Willy the photo. "Is this what you're talking about? The star elders?"

Willy looks at the blurry photo. "I always thought they were silly stories."

"Were they taken by force?"

"I don't think so. They went on their own free will, convinced that it was time to leave because it was no longer safe."

"Why wouldn't it be safe?"

"I have a feeling we're going to find out."

George and Colleen stomp around the corner. George holds out a brochure. "This says the villages are occupied."

"I was interested in buying some jewelry." Colleen points at a jeweler in the brochure, "He's not home. Nobody is."

Willy walks back to the van. George declares that this was the worst tour he's ever been on.

"Don't worry, you'll get your money back." Willy opens the door to the van. "Not that it's going to matter."

"What's that supposed to mean?"

Just then something occurs to Alan. Willy was left behind. His friends and family have gone.

Willy looks into Alan with his one eye that seems to hold

more wisdom than all of them put together. "Let's go start your car."

The drive back down the mesa is quiet. Alan tries to piece together the events but still can't grasp what has transpired. Willy thinks the Hopi have been willingly rescued by aliens or 'star elders.' Why does he think they were rescued? Who are these 'star elders'? Alan doesn't have a clue but doesn't doubt that the UFO last night has something to do with it. Whatever happened, Willy is alarmed and thinks we should be too.

Willy hooks up the jumper cables to Alan's car and signals that he's ready. After a couple of turns, the engine starts. Alan sighs with relief. He was beginning to think he was in a weird vortex, and he would never leave.

Willy shuts the hood of the Subaru and gives Alan a thumbs-up. This triggers another peculiar feeling in Alan, even more intense than the previous time. Willy shares the same experience—the sense of knowing someone you've never met.

Willy adjusts his eye patch. "Where you headed?"

"Back to Albuquerque. I've had enough adventure for now." Alan pushes his glasses up. "What did you mean, exactly, when you said something was going down?"

"The end times. I think something major will impact everyone on the planet."

"You really think those people were rescued by aliens? I mean, who will believe that?"

"It doesn't matter what people believe."

Alan feels a sudden urge to be back on campus in the safety

of his dorm room or to go home and sit with his dad on the front porch. His body shivers. "I don't want this to be the end."

"Everything has an end."

Foo Fighters

Alan gathers empty soda cans, popcorn bags, and random trash out of his car. Two figures walk in his direction through a mirage of heat and dust. He cups his hands over his glasses to block the sun. Two boys with backpacks approach him. The tall, trim boy looks to be a few years younger than Alan. The short one, wearing a red hat, has a round face and plump cheeks and looks several years younger.

"Hey, there," says Alan. The boys avoid eye contact. "Do you need some help?"

The tall boy replies, "We're good."

Alan gets in his car and drives away then looks back at the boys in the blazing heat. "Hey, do you need a ride? I'm headin' to town."

The boys look at each other for approval. The older one shrugs his shoulders. "Okay."

"Are you going home?"

"We have no home," answers the younger boy with the red hat. He climbs into the back seat. The older one gets in the front seat and looks back at the younger boy. "I told you to let me do the talking."

"Are you from the village?" Alan says driving away. "No one was there."

The boys remain silent. Alan looks at the younger boy in the rearview mirror. "What are your names? I'm Alan."

"Chuchip," says the older boy. "That's my brother, Hania."

"Cool names. Why aren't you with your family?"

"He was scared," answers Chuchip.

"No, I wasn't," snaps Hania.

Alan sees him wipe away tears.

"That's cool. It's okay to be scared," says Alan. "I saw something last night that scared the crap out of me. I have the lump on my head to prove it. Maybe you saw it, too." Alan looks at Chuchip for a reaction.

"We're going into town," says Chuchip.

"Do you have someone to take care of you?"

"I'm 17. I don't need anyone to take care of me."

"Okay, that's cool. I'm 20, and I do need someone to take of me." Alan snorts, but the boys' faces are expressionless.

Chuchip looks at Alan. "Where are you headed?"

"Albuquerque. That's where I go to school."

"We'll go there then."

"Ahh, I don't think so. That's, like, illegal. I don't want to go to jail for kidnapping."

"It's not like you're taking us by force," says Chuchip.

"Look, it's not going to happen." Alan turns onto the paved road. "So...what's going on? I mean, did your parents go with these star people?"

"We should've gone with them." Chuchip frowns and looks out the window. "Hania was being difficult."

"They're aliens!" Hania blurts sharply.

Alan looks at him in the review mirror. "Little green men, like, aliens?"

"No, they look human, mostly," says Chuchip. "Said they were taking us to their planet."

"They abducted everyone in your village?"

"And taking them to some planet. But we'll never know, right?" says Chuchip to his brother.

"I don't want to get between you and your brother or anything, but I'm with Hania, I wouldn't have gone. That's just crazy. Look, I need to get some things in town, and then you guys will be okay, right?"

"Sure." Chuchip crosses his arms and sighs.

Alan parks in front of the convenience store. He looks at his phone. He missed three calls from his parents. "Alright, then." He looks shamefully at the boys, uncomfortable with dropping them off like two strays. "Good luck with everything." The boys get out and walk down the street.

Inside the convenience store, Alan finds his favorite popcorn and soda. The store attendant has his face glued to the little TV that sits on the counter. A reporter talks about the flood of phone calls regarding strange lights in the sky.

Alan puts the popcorn, soda, and a roadmap on the counter. "Do you mind turning that up?" The journalist has a British accent with footage of green and red lights in the sky. "Where is that?" Alan says.

"Somewhere in England." He rings up the total. "$12.50, please."

"England?"

"Yeah." He gives Alan his change. "But this has been all over... sightings everywhere."

Breaking news from India interrupts. Iran, Iraq, and Saudi Arabia were under attack. The perpetrator is an unknown assailant with weapons of unknown origin. Russians are suspect.

Alan's face pales. He plays a message from his mom in the car. "Alan, we're not sure if you've heard or seen the news, but could you please give us a call? We just want to know you're alright." He calls his parents but can't get through. There's an old pay phone on the side of the store. He picks up the receiver and hears a dial tone. This is the first time he's ever used a pay phone, and he hasn't dialed the landline in ten years. After he dials, he follows the instructions and digs in his pockets for change and inserts .50 cents.

KABOOM! Alan covers his head and falls to the ground. Windows blow into the convenience store. They shatter on vehicles. Broken glass is everywhere. A terrible, high-pitched sound rings in his head. He covers his ears with his hands, but that makes it worse. There's mass hysteria on the street. People run every which way. Through the chaos, Alan can only see muted screams and terrified faces. There's a pungent smell. Alan covers his nose and mouth. The smell makes him sick, and when he sees where the smell is coming from, he pukes. Bodies are burning. He wants to run away from the horrible sight and horrific tone in his head. The attendant from the convenience store frantically runs out with his hands covering his ears. He's instantly killed. Something from the sky targets those who run around trying to escape the maddening sound. All of them are killed, leaving behind burning, black bodies.

In the chaos, he sees Chuchip and his brother crouch down on the ground, also covering their ears. Alan wants to run to his car to escape the torturous sound, but intense fear paralyzes him. His inability to move is keeping him alive. He looks up and discovers the source of the sound. Strange, almost invisible, spheres hover above the buildings and trees, blending into the sky with only the slightest detection of waves. Before they eject their death ray, the spheres flash into a ball of blinding, neon light.

Military helicopters fly above and surround the spheres. They shoot missiles into these foreign, invisible invaders. Alan wants to gash his ears out to make it stop. He screams to the boys, and his voice sounds like it's underwater. "Stay down!"

Smoke rises from the cashier's body. He's burnt and chard beyond recognition. Alan's car is a mere ten feet away, but it might as well be a mile.

Willy, the tour guide, frantically waves his arms. "Alan! Over here!" Chuchip pulls on his arm. Alan looks up when missiles fire into the spheres.

"No! Don't run!" Alan hopes his voice doesn't sound as muffled to them as it does to himself. "Don't move!" Alan repeats, unable to say anything else.

KABOOM! A helicopter is on fire and crash-lands on a building about twenty yards away. A screaming girl comes running out of the building. She gets incinerated. Alan and the boys fall to the ground and cover their heads from the explosion and the fiery debris.

"Get down!" Willy warns.

Chuchip and Hania get down on their stomachs and crawl, military style, towards the van. The boys stay as low to the ground as possible. Willy helps them into the back of the van one at a time. Alan remains frozen.

"Alan, get the hell in here!" says Willy. Alan gets on his stomach, and there's another explosion. Military missiles finally have luck, and the spheres disappear. Willy pulls him up and swiftly forces him into the van, slamming the door shut. There's no light, and Alan's eyes slowly adjust. Cardboard covers up the windows, sealed with duct tape. They're finally free from the ringing noise. Alan feels dazed and nauseous.

Chuchip coughs from the smoke and fumes. "Get us out of here!"

"We have to wait," says Willy.

Finally, Alan notices. The van is stocked with weapons. Different sizes of crossbows, military rifles, tons of ammo, explosives, and camping gear surround them. "This is not your tour van. Is this even legal?"

Willy looks at Alan with his good eye. He appears quite different in this context. A person you don't want to mess with. "Legal? Yes and no. Mostly no. This is the van I live in. These are weapons I've collected over the years after I came back from Vietnam."

Hania, without warning, vomits all over himself. Willy hands him a towel. "I got sick, too, Hania, in my first battle.

This is different, I know. It's hard to compare this to anything, except when Europeans invaded our country, and it was the first time we saw weaponry that exceeded imagination. They were strange aliens to us. Like that, this is beyond anything you ever imagined. Whoever they are, they want to get rid of us."

"My Mom called about this. This is some kind of invasion. And reports...something about UFO sightings all over the world, like what I saw last night. What the hell are those things shooting at us?" Alan takes a deep breath and wipes the sweat and dirt off his glasses with the bottom of his t-shirt.

Willy shifts his patch and rubs his eye. "I don't know. Some kind of crazy technology, like, foo fighters."

"That's, like, a band."

"Foo fighters were mysterious UFO sightings that the allies reported during WWII."

"That went around killing everything?" asks Chuchip.

"Military thought they were advanced Nazi technology, perhaps even extraterrestrial."

"They certainly didn't look terrestrial," says Alan. "Do you think the people or the aliens who came to your village did this?"

Chuchip takes off his backpack. "I don't know."

Willy removes a cardboard cover and peers out the window. "I think it's safe to go out there."

"What for?" Alan asks.

"Those foo fighters, whatever you want to call them, have been destroyed, but before they come back, which they most likely will, we need to get supplies."

Alan has a headache and rubs his head. "Supplies for you and your stockpile of weapons?"

"For you...for all of us."

"Look. I'm not going to be in your little army. I'm getting out of here and back to school."

"You heard the news. Something is happening globally. We need to be ready." He opens the van door and steps out. "The military has limited power against whatever it is. It's every man for himself, so we need to help each other if we're going to get through this."

The boys hop out. Alan slides the van door shut behind them. "This is just crazy! You're crazy! We'll let the military take care of this. Things will go back to normal."

Willy heads into the convenience store, pushing a cart down the aisle. He stops at the peanut butter and looks at the boys.

"Our true white brothers returned like they said they would. The visitor you saw saved them from rapture. Our people stood by their promise and walked a righteous path. We were left behind." He looks away. "I don't know. Maybe there's a reason." His eye refocuses. "We have two options. Die as cowards or die fighting with honor." He places six jars of peanut butter in the cart.

"Who are we fighting?" Chuchip asks.

Willy pushes his cart down the next aisle. "Those who want us dead. If I die fighting, at least my spirit will know I tried."

Alan rubs his forehead. "Both of those options suck. There must be another option that doesn't involve dying!"

"You heard," says Willy. "The whole world is under siege."

Hania grabs a box of Kit-Kat bars, and Willy yanks them out of his hands. "We need things like rice, beans, potatoes. Things that will keep us alive."

"What about things that will make us happy?"

"You got me there." Willy gives them back.

Other survivors, with frantic expressions on their faces and blood dripping from their ears, wander in and walk around the aisles grabbing milk, eggs, and anything else they can get their hands on.

"Get things that won't spoil," Willy instructs as Alan grabs milk from the refrigerator, "like dried fruits, nuts, canned goods."

"Okay, okay, sorry. I'm new at this. I'll drink it right away," Alan says, putting the milk in his cart. "I haven't craved milk since I was a kid."

"Get all the medicine you can, also. Never mind. I'll be in charge of that. I know what to get. Meet back at the van in five minutes."

The store owner lies dead with a gunshot wound to his head behind the counter. A rifle lies by his side. Hania nearly trips on him. "Why did he do that?"

"To make it stop," Alan says pointing to his ears. "I might have done the same thing, had I a gun."

They stock the van with boxes of food, water, medicine, and supplies. "Okay, now what?" Alan leans against the van to rest.

"We get as much gas as we can. We need gas cans."

Willy and the boys walk across the street which now looks

like a war zone. A building is on fire, and the helicopter hangs on the edge of the roof. The tail end breaks away and lands on the ground. They zig-zag around charred bodies and step through windowless doors, crunching on broken glass as they walk. "Be careful," says Willy. "Don't slip and fall on this."

They fill each gas container and tie them onto the roof of the van. Willy inspects and secures the rope. "This is only for backup if it gets to that point. We need this van for as long as possible."

Alan checks his phone. "I'm going to call my parents."

"Make it quick."

Alan dials hoping and praying they answer. The phone barely rings once, and someone picks up. "Hello?"

"Dad?"

"Alan! Are you okay? Where are you?"

"Yeah, I'm fine. I'm with some people. What's going on there?"

"I was commuting back from Philly when it hit. Everyone heard a crazy, loud boom. Our heads were filled with a high-pitched ring that's hard to describe."

"I know exactly what you're talking about. It was the same here."

"Your mom and I are okay. We don't know if it's some kind of foreign attack."

"Dad, this is a foreign attack, but it's not another country. It's alien."

"That's ridiculous."

"I don't have time to explain because I gotta go, Dad. I called to say I love you. Tell Mom I'm okay, and I love you both."

"Alan, where are you going?"

"Somewhere safe, until this blows over."

"Alan!"

"Get as much food and water as you can. Take Mom to the cabin. This could happen again."

"Yeah, we were just talking about that. I'm glad you're okay, Alan. We love you, too."

Alan hangs up and runs back to the van.

"They're alive?" Willy asks.

"Yeah. My dad said that Philadelphia was hit. They don't know what's going on, though. Maybe this is going to blow over."

Willy slides the van door shut. "This was only round one." He drives over to Alan's car, and the front windshield is cracked.

"How much gas do you have?" Willy asks.

"Full tank. Should be good to Albuquerque. Is that where we're heading?"

"Albuquerque is as good a place as any. Do you know anyone there?"

"I haven't met that many people yet. Except..."

"Except what?"

"This girl. She also disappeared last week with her cousin or brother."

Chuchip bites into a Kit-Kat. "That's weird."

"Yeah, it's weird, and I was the last person who saw them."

Hania curls up and sleeps on the Indian blanket and pil-lows. "Is he gonna be alright?" Alan asks before getting into his car.

Willy looks back through the rearview mirror. "He's sleep-ing it off."

"Sleeping what off?"

"The shock."

Adam and Eve

A young couple, looking disheveled, walks into The Road-runner. Beverly sets two glasses of water for them on a table and two menus. "Here. Make yourself comfortable."

Today was her day off, but she hasn't taken one since Anah disappeared. It's unusually slow at the Roadrunner this morn-ing, and Beverly assumes it's because of the strange onslaught of attacks. People are afraid. Everyone speculates who's to blame, but Beverly knows better.

"Is it okay if we don't order anything? We just need a break from driving," says the young man.

Beverly looks the couple over. They look stressed and like they haven't bathed in several days. "Is everything okay?"

"Been driving for several days," says the young man.

"Did you come from one of the cities that was attacked?"

"Portland, Maine. We were camping before the attack. When we saw what they did, we decided to drive until we found a safe place. We ended up here."

"Do you have any money?"

"We can't get into our bank account or any ATM's. When I went to the bank, they said their whole system is down. I told them how much money I had and that I needed to withdraw. They wouldn't allow it, so we went to another branch, but it was closed."

"I'm glad you're okay." Beverly looks at the young lady about the same age as Anah. "I'm Beverly. Order anything you want. It's on the house."

"That's very generous. Thank you," she says. "I'm Eve and this is Adam."

"You're joking? Adam and Eve?"

He cracks a smile. "Jokes on us."

"I'll give you a moment to decide." Beverly returns to the kitchen.

A regular, who comes in every morning for a breakfast burrito and coffee, walks into the restaurant carrying an old, box TV.

The restaurant owner, Harry, walks over to him. "Wha-chya got there, Dan?"

"I brought my old TV. Can I plug it in there?" He motions to the countertop, a few stools down from Adam and Eve. Perspiration drips down his face.

Beverly hands him a glass of lemon water. "Hi, Dan. Brought the news to us? Not sure if anyone wants to hear it."

"I don't think it'll work without cable." Harry protests.

"Of course it will." Dan takes a sip of water between breaths, "I have an antenna. That's how I watch TV. You don't need no cable! Airwaves are better these days. And It's free for Pete's sake."

Harry waves his hand and says, "We don't want it on, Dan." Dan finds a channel that captures everyone's attention with a breaking, live report. There's a lot of chatter and commotion in the newsroom, and no one is sitting at the desk. The camera captures the bewilderment of people in the newsroom, shuffling about. Dan, Beverly, Harry, Adam, and Eve stare with nervous anticipation. Dan takes another drink of lemon water and wipes the sweat off his forehead.

Finally, a male newscaster sits down to face the camera. "We would like to--" He stops talking while someone whispers in his ear. "We want everyone, please, to remain calm, and to listen closely. Everyone is asked to please, for the love of God, remain indoors, preferably in your homes. Do not go outside or make yourself visible on the streets or in your yards. Do not go to your schools. Do not go to your jobs until further notice. All planes have been grounded and airports have been shut. Border crossings are closed. We have some disturbing footage that we decided not to release because it's too graphic..." The newscaster stops before he continues. "We are waiting to hear a live report from the president, but we've lost communication." Someone walks on camera again and hands him a paper, whispering something in his ear. The news reporter's face turns white. "I'm sorry to report that...We've just got word..." He's unable to finish his sentence. Another reporter comes to take his place and attempts to give the report.

"We have terrible news," he begins slowly and carefully. "We just got word that the president was rushed to the hospital. A reliable source has reported that he was dead on arrival." He pauses to listen from his earpiece. "The cause of death is unknown. We will keep you posted. These attacks, we believe, we know now, that these attacks are not from any leader or country that we know of. These attacks are from an alien race." He pauses and stares seriously into the camera. "They are not human, and we don't know what they want. What we do know is that they are killing us. The military, not just the U.S. but all militaries around the world, are engaged in combat with these foreign, otherworldly invaders. For the first time man is united, as one race, fighting against a common enemy." Even through the little box television, the fright on his face is clear. "May God bless us all."

Beverly hears a glass fall behind her. She turns around, and Dan is hunched over, holding his abdomen in pain. He falls to the floor.

"He's not breathing," Harry says feeling for his breath.

"Is he choking?" Beverly says in fright.

Harry feels for Dan's pulse. "He has no pulse!"

Beverly runs to the landline and dials 911. But there's no connection.

"I'll try to resuscitate him!" Harry opens Dan's mouth.

"Wait!" Beverly runs to him. "Don't touch him!" Beverly picks up the water glass off the floor that Dan was drinking from. She looks to Eve, who's getting ready to drink from her glass and dashes over to her, knocking the glass out of her hand and onto the floor. "Stop! Don't touch that water."

Harry comes to his feet. "Have you lost your mind?"

"I don't know, maybe I have. But Dan... he was fine, and then he fell over dead after drinking water."

Adam slides his water glass far away.

"Beverly, you're scaring the customers. Maybe you need to take the rest of the day off."

"I'm scaring the customers? Dan just dropped dead, and what about what we just heard on the news?"

The TV interrupts with an emergency broadcast. The kind you normally hear as a test, but this one is not a test. There aren't any newscasters reporting; however, there is a recorded message that repeats: Return to your homes. Don't leave your home unless you have an emergency. Do not drink any public water. Drink only bottled water and/or well water.

Beverly points to the screen. "I'm not crazy! They've contaminated our water." She wipes the spill off the floor and throws away the towel.

"Why are they doing this?" Eve cries.

"We need to leave now," Adam says.

Beverly turns the TV off. "Where would you go? We were instructed to stay home."

Eve is crying and wipes tears off her cheeks. "I don't know. We don't have anywhere to go."

"You can come with me. I live alone, and I wouldn't mind. I can make us something to eat."

Adam looks appears anxious. Eve gives him a pleading stare. "Alright," he says. "That's very gracious of you, Beverly. Thank you. We'll stay just for tonight." Eve looks relieved.

Harry takes off his white apron and turns the sign from open to closed. "What about Dan?"

"I'll help you move him," says Adam.

Harry sighs and both his hands go to his head. "I can't have him here. 911 doesn't respond."

"He lives down the street," says Beverly. "We'll take him home until this gets sorted out."

A Path

Beverly places dinner plates on the table with the stir fry she quickly put together.

"I like your house," says Eve. "It has a cool vibe."

Beverly chuckles. "Whatever I could find at a thrift shop or a giveaway on the side of the road kind of vibe." Beverly looks at Alan who's not listening and hasn't participated in any conversation since they arrived. He behaves disturbingly and seems deeply distracted.

"Help yourself to the shower. You can use the one in my daughter's room."

Eve stabs her fork into a carrot. "Where's your daughter?"

"She's..." Beverly tries to speak, but there's a sudden lump in her throat. She swallows hard. "Hopefully, somewhere safe."

"We appreciate your hospitality, Beverly," says Adam, and Beverly nearly jumps at the sudden sound of his voice. "We're not going to stay long. After we eat and bathe, we'll be on our way." Eve furrows her brow.

"It's not safe to leave, Adam. Where will you go?"

"Beverly, we haven't been exactly upfront about everything." Eve crosses her arms.

"Eve, you agreed that we would keep it between us." Adam rolls his eyes.

Beverly looks between them. "I don't want to cause any problems between you two."

"It's Adam. Not you, Beverly. He's experiencing something that I don't understand, but I've been willing, so far, to go along with it." Adam lets out a harsh sigh. Eve continues. "Apparently, he's been following a path—in his mind."

He stands and raises his voice. "It's very real and very intense."

Beverly leads them to the living room. "A path? What do you mean exactly?"

"Alright, I'll explain it, even though I didn't want to." He paces to the other side of the room. "It's, like, internal."

"It's not a real, physical path?"

"Well, it's that, also. But I know where to go without knowing."

"So, it's based on a feeling?"

"It does feel instinctual. Sometimes I hear sounds that help guide me."

"Like a voice?"

He shakes his head. "More like music... a flute, a horn, or a trumpet. It was loud and clear when we drove to The Roadhouse, so I stopped. I think because this was supposed to happen..finding you. Now it's pulling me again, and it's time to move on. You're thinking I'm a lunatic."

"No. No, I'm not. Believe me. I don't think that you're crazy."

"He hasn't slept since this started," says Eve.

"You're not tired?"

"I've never felt so awake in my life."

"This internal path brought you here, all the way from Maine?"

"I think the closer I get, the stronger it becomes. Now, it's the strongest It's ever been."

"How will you know when you finally get there?"

"I'm starting to get an image in my mind."

"Can you draw it?"

"I can try."

Beverly finds paper and a pencil in her kitchen drawer and hands it to Adam. He begins to sketch something out. He moves the pencil up and down, to the right and left. After many attempts, Beverly's face lights up.

Eve moves in closer and looks straight at Beverly. "What's wrong? Do you recognize something?"

She finds a photograph book from the bookshelf titled, New Mexico. She quickly flips through the pages and points to a picture. "Is this it?"

Adam taps his finger several times on the page. "That's where I'm heading. That's it!"

"Then you are close. That's the Glorieta mesa. I can take you there."

Rescue Mission

Victor listens intently to AmanKi before he and the other Keepers are dismissed. He doesn't want to screw this one up. He feels unusually nervous. There's no room for mistakes or unnecessary risks.

"We have a very small window to complete this mission before the Simerin are on to us. MinnEnKi met with the U.S. president. He panicked and made regretful negotiations with the Simerin. Before he died, he reversed course, giving us the government's cooperation. Therefore, when encountering military, they are our allies. We negotiated a World Order Militia. They are having some success against the Simerin's weapons. Be vigilant. Stay on guard. There's mass confusion with the WOM since they didn't know their command, but they are getting organized. Most importantly, head straight back to the ship when signaled. We cannot risk a failed mission, lose Chantallah or the ship—our only way back to NeuMonah. If this should happen..." AmanKi pauses and looks into all of the eager Keepers. "You know where to go."

AmanKi refers to the secret chambers that could house thousands of humans. An underground city awaits with food, water, and medical supplies, in each chamber.

"Our Mission is to save Chantallah in this area," says MinnEnKi. "By now, they know who they are."

Victor steps to the front of the group. "Do the Chantallah know we are here and that it's time?"

"The more sensitive ones know. They lead the way for the others."

"Many Adamah have already been killed," voices a concerned Keeper, Bahliah.

"That's why we need to act swiftly and covertly." MinnenKi tightens his jaw. "I have confidence. We can save the Adamah."

Like bees leaving their hive, transports disperse from the ship to their assigned locations. Victor converts his nervousness into confidence. The rescue mission depends on it. It's for the future good of all beings, not just for those on Earth. The Chantallah are in route, with loved ones in tow. They have no idea why they are migrating to a location that pulls them like a magnet. After landing his transport in the cover of the woods, Victor opens a large gate to a field where Amanda grazes. He whistles, and she perks up her head and ears and trots to Victor in a warm greeting. "I miss you, too." Victor caresses her neck. "It's time for you to go, Amanda. I must go now. I'll leave the gate open for you." Victor walks away, and Amanda follows. "I'm sorry, Amanda, you can't come with me." Amanda stomps her hoof in the dry earth to protest.

Victor makes his way back through the woods. Two people in their twenties, a young man and a woman, rest and eat an orange under a ponderosa, unaware of Victor.

"Hello," he says gently to avoid startling them.

"Sorry if we're trespassing. We'll be on our way." The young couple stands and collects their backpacks.

"It's okay. Please, don't leave. I'm here to help you. To bring you to safety. My name is Victor. What are your names?"

"I'm Jason," says the young man.

"I'm Kelly. What are we doing here?"

"follow me." Victor leads them down the path. The hatch door to his transport slides open from the seamless, reflective side of the craft.

Jason hesitates. He doesn't want to follow Victor into the craft. "Kelly, I was willing to follow you up to this point, but I can't go any farther."

"It's okay, Jason. This is it," She says.

Victor uses a stronger approach since he doesn't have time to settle debates. "If you stay, you will perish. We are here to rescue you."

"Listen to your heart," Kelly pleads. "If you can't, then trust me."Jason reluctantly boards the craft, and the door slides closed behind him.

Victor shakes Jason's hand. "Excellent. Now, let us go rescue more people!"

Victor flies the craft low above the tree line. He stares at his monitor that detects body heat and finds a group of four. A woman and her three daughters walk in the field that leads to his house. He lands the craft and exits the port in the field. They all stare at him unsure if what they see is real.

"Hello," says Victor. "Do you know why you are here?"

They stare at him without expression.

"You're here to leave your planet. If you stay you will not survive."

"We came from Pennsylvania," says the woman, "Our car broke down in Texas."

"We're hungry and tired," says the youngest daughter.

"My husband didn't make it," the woman cries. "He drank the water."

"I will take you to the ship," says Victor. "You'll receive care there. I have water in my transport. Come meet the others."

"Up there?" The daughter points to the sky with her deep brown eyes.

"Yes. We don't have much time."

"Hurry!" Kelly instructs with her arm. "There are others we need to rescue!"

Crash Course

Alan drives across the New Mexico State line. He looks at his gasometer. Half a tank. Enough to get back to Albuquerque. Reluctantly, he follows Willy down a long dirt road that has no end in sight. He fumbles with his new map. It takes up the front seat and most of the dash. "Where the hell are you going, Willy?"

They pass a sign that says, Devil's Canyon. Alan slams on his brakes and slides to a halt. The van comes to a full stop and parks off the side of the road that overlooks a large, rocky canyon. A raven rides the warm draft coming up from the bottom of the canyon. The sun reflects off his ruby-black back. Through the dust, Alan steps out of his car and looks down into the narrow canyon. "What are we doing here?"

"I need to go over some things with you boys." Willy opens both doors to the back of the van. "So, we're prepared for what comes next. I have a lot of arsenals that you need to get familiar with. If something should happen to me, you three are my beneficiaries. Everything I own is in this van."

Willy sets up several dead logs on a rock. "This is the M4 Carbine. He's very special. I call him Herc, after Hercules. He's good for most situations, short range and up to 500 meters, both semi and fully automatic. It's equipped with night vision and a grenade launcher. This magazine," Willy pops one in. "It has 30 rounds. It's important to remember so you don't get killed giving up your position." Willy looks through the scope with his eye. Every shot rips through a heap of dead wood. He hands Herc to Chip and instructs him on posture and how to hold it, so the recoil doesn't blow out his shoulder. Chip and Hania take turns firing the M4, blasting through the wood targets.

Willy hands Alan another rifle, but he declines. "I don't see how this is going to do anything. You saw what I saw. Those bodies were burned to a crisp—in seconds. We might as well use bows and arrows."

"Maybe you're right. But we don't know what we'll encounter." Willy slides open the barrel and loads a grenade. He steadies the rifle into his upper chest and fires. Smoke and dust explode on the desert floor about 300 meters away. "I would like to see what could survive that."

Alan crosses his arms. "Is that what you used in Vietnam?"

"That would be the M16, what I used then. It's almost the same." Willy holds up his rifle. "Uses different cartridges, like the M855 cartridge. It will penetrate through body armor."

Chuchip picks up a magazine. "Those are for the M16. Don't get them confused."

"Too late," says Alan.

"Sorry. This crash course will have to be enough for now. We can't hang out here too long."

"Thanks, Willy, for not treating me like a little kid," Hania says.

"In battle, you're no less a man than us if you're prepared." Willy opens an artillery box with several M16 rifles, hundreds of magazines, and another crate full of AK-47s "Yep. We don't know our enemy, yet, but this will do for now." Willy's eye lights up. Even his patch looks delighted. He has prepared for this his whole life. "Don't use these against those foo fighters, though. We saw how they withstood the bullets from the military. If we come face to face with these coward aliens, we'll Rambo up."

The young men look into Willy's eye. Alan pushes his glasses up the bridge of his nose. "Rambo up?"

Willy fires the M16 across the canyon, his thoughts haunted by the images of his friends' bodies on fire. He doesn't want revenge. Something deeper and deadlier grows in the pit of his stomach. Chuchip, Hania, and Alan join him and shoot their weapons across the canyon. When they empty their magazine, Willy puts out his fist. The boys put their fists on top. "We can do this together," Willy says with a tear in his eye.

"Together," repeats Chuchip and Hania.

Alan looks at the men. "Together!" A feeling stirs deep

inside him. He's never experienced camaraderie before, and a spark grows inside him.

They call out a series of hollers like warriors going into battle. Willy sings a Navajo song. Chuchip and Hania recognize some of the meanings. It will bring them good luck and protection as warriors.

On the Mesa

Beverly's thoughts melt into her tea, like the honey she stirs, unable to decipher what actions are needed for her survival, including the young couple she's taken under her wing. MinnEnki warned her about the possibility of a Simerin attack. She wishes she had a clearer picture of what was happening between the Simerin and Monahdah. Staying put and waiting might be the best option.

Eve looks over at Adam. "It makes me nervous when you're this quiet."

"I'm thinking," he says. "Beverly, can I turn the TV on?"

"Okay."

The television is blank when Adam turns it on. "No reception," he says.

Beverly takes the remote and flips through the channels. The lights go out and the TV shuts off. "Now we're without power. I have a backup generator. We should be fine." She lights a candle on the mantle.

Adam looks at his phone. "They've cut off communication completely."

Eve sits on the edge of the sofa. "Who exactly are you referring to?"

"Whoever's doing this." Adam points to the picture in the book of the mesa. "I think you should take us to this place. We need to leave. The sooner the better."

"You said we could leave in the morning." Eve sounds like she's about to cry. "I'm exhausted, and it's cold out there."

"I'm sorry, Eve."

"Alright. I can take you there, even though I think it's a bad idea. We have a few hours of daylight left. If we're going to do this, we should go now." Beverly grabs backpacks from a closet. "We should pack food and water."

Adam starts filling water bottles. "Is this water okay? The emergency broadcast said to only drink bottled water."

"My well hasn't been contaminated. I was drinking it all morning, and I'm fine."

The underbelly of clouds turns orange and pink—the shadows of the piñons, junipers, and Chamisa stretch oblong across the desert floor. Beverly relies on her poor memory as she drives up to the top of the mesa. A few yellow leaves still hold on to the cottonwoods. Chamisa seeds blow in the wind. She navigates the old dirt roads, seldom used by anyone besides a few ranchers, and prays her old Corolla will make it. She's not sure if it's necessary to take Adam to the Monahdah compound and doubts there will be anyone there. She pushes away thoughts of abandonment and doesn't allow her feelings to cloud her judgment. This is what she is meant to do and has faith in her ability to lead these people, and herself to safety. She stops at the gate.

Adam looks around at the enclosed property. "What do we do now?"

Beverly grabs her backpack and opens her door. "We walk."

Eve crosses her arms in protest. "How far is that? And what exactly do we do once we get there? I have a terrible feeling about this."

"I estimate that it's another 45 minutes or so on foot. I don't exactly know what we do next. I'm not being guided by some internal force, so, Adam why don't you answer that question?"

Adam closes his eyes, and for a moment, there's complete silence. A sudden swift breeze dances through the dry grasses. Adam points. "This way."

After twenty minutes of following Adam through the field, Eve stumbles over a small log hidden in the grass. She stops to clean herself off. "This is crazy. I don't know why I'm going along with all this." She points to Beverly. "No offense, Beverly, but I don't know you, and Adam hears things in his head. Maybe that's all it is — in his head!"

"You're right, Eve," says Adam. "This all could be in my head. I might be crazy. But I wasn't crazy before all this alien stuff happened—when you trusted me!"

Eve stares at Beverly. "What about her?"

"I'm helping you, aren't I? I didn't have to drive you up here and walk around on the top of this mesa."

Eve crosses her arms. "Where's your daughter? Huh? And

why aren't you with her? You didn't even try calling her to see if she's okay?"

"Eve, that isn't any of our business."

"It's okay," Beverly holds up her hand in resolution. "I'll explain."

A lone coyote calls out in the distance and Adam looks around with a worried look. With the remaining sunlight, he sets his site on the dark tree line to the northwest. "We are way too exposed out here. It doesn't matter, right now, where Beverly's daughter is."

"It will take but a minute. I can explain," Beverly says firmly.

"We have to get to that tree line, like, now!"

"Why are you talking so loudly? You're practically yelling," says Eve.

Beverly takes out her water bottle. "We should try to be quiet. We can be heard just as easily as spotted."

"I'm sorry," Adam says in a loud whisper. "It's so loud! I can barely hear you or myself."

"What do you hear?" Beverly takes a drink of water.

"It's so loud, like trumpets. It's maddening!" He holds his head.

Beverly returns the water bottle into the backpack. "Okay. We can hear you fine, so please try not to yell."

"I can't make you believe in something I don't even understand, but all I ask is that you have a little trust in me." Adam sighs and takes her hand. "I love you, Eve."

Eve's face softens, and she hugs him. "I do trust you." She stares at him for a moment. "Whatever this is that's happening to us... I came this far." She searches for the right words. "I love you, too, Adam. Even though I don't understand. I'm with you." Eve looks over at Beverly. "But I still want to know her deal."

"I will tell you everything..." Beverly sighs.

"What's that!" Adam interrupts and points to the sky. Like fireflies, lights fall from the sky one after the other, right over the tree line. "Get down!"

They huddle on the ground and spy the lights. The crafts hover for a moment and disappear into the clouds.

Beverly looks up. "Adam's right. We must get to the woods."

Eve stays crouched down on her knees. "I don't think we should get any closer to those things."

"We're sitting ducks." Adam points. "If we get to the first group of piñons, we're halfway there."

Beverly swings the backpack over her shoulders and tightens the straps. "They're here to help."

"You don't know that."

Adam can't take it anymore and runs to the first group of piñons for cover. Beverly follows right behind. Eve must run to catch up, and they reach the first group of piñon trees. Winded, Eve whispers loudly. "Thanks for waiting!"

"The music in my head is urging us to keep going." Rustling sounds and loud breathing behind the piñon trees silence them.

They cautiously walk around to the other side of the trees. A horse raises his head.

Eve grabs onto Adam's arm. "Holy crap, that scared me. What's he doing out here all alone?"

Beverly puts her hand out, and the horse smells her palm. "I know you. This is Victor's horse." Adam and Eve stare. "Victor is my daughter's boyfriend. He comes from another planet and those aircrafts belong to them. They're here to help. That's my story. I told you it wouldn't take a minute."

"There're others? The ones that want to help us and the ones that want to kill us."

"Yes. We need to get to those trees before we run into the ones that want to kill us."

Eve looks doubtful. "It's quite far. A good two hundred yards. Should we sprint the whole way?"

"Shit!" Adam pulls Eve down with him and ducks down. "Doesn't look like that's a good one."

Beverly conceals herself behind the tree branches.

Adam points with his eyes. To the west, 100 yards away, a figure with a drawn weapon approaches them. He sniffs the air and follows their scent as he lurks through the tall grass. The sun dips behind the horizon, and the figure's body and face are concealed in shadow.

Beverly sinks into herself and covers her mouth for fear she might scream. Eve closes her eyes tight and prays. Adam doesn't know what frightens him more, this alien hunting for them, or the fact that the music in his head has suddenly stopped. He barely breathes and doesn't move a muscle. Then he knows what it is he must do—what he was always supposed to do. This clarity reveals to him something that reaches into the internal depth of his soul, beyond courage, and his body is filled with something he can't describe—his purpose.

In Jeopardy

Victor scans the sky. He drops down and hovers over the tree line. A large group of Chantallah have gathered in the woods. Victor worries the group could attract Simerin and increase the risk of the mission. He spots two Simerin scouts, hunting for Adamah, and to his dismay, three Chantallah, oblivious to the danger they're in, argue amongst themselves in the field. Engaging will create unwanted attention and put the group in the woods and everyone already on board, in jeopardy. He must stick to the plan. When he realizes who it is, Victor calls into the Keeper's outpost station. "We have a situation!"

A Simerin craft approach. Beverly and the two companions will be caught off guard if they don't get into the coverage of the woods. He could create a distraction and give them time. He was told to work covertly. This could put the whole mission in jeopardy.

Victor hovers in the clouds. "I have Beverly in view. What should I do?"

MinnEnki drops down for his last run. "They're heading to the woods. Create a diversion!"

"Yes, Sir!"

Victor drops down. The Sim fighter immediately fires.

Victor makes a hard left, and, like cat and mouse, they follow him across the desert.

Ashes and Dust

"I must do this." Adam stands and looks at Eve. "I love you." He steps out of the trees. Eve grabs his arm, but Beverly forces her back.

"What are you doing?" Beverly doesn't answer Eve because there's no more time to argue. She knows this is their only chance.

Adam takes ahold of Amanda's mane, swings his leg over her back, and yells, "HAH!" She gallops across the field, and Adam's long, wavy hair bounces on his back. Amanda's long, white tail whips through the air behind them, an image that will be forever in Eve's memory. This unexpected activity creates the perfect diversion. The Sim takes the bait, turns, and runs in the direction of the horse and rider.

"It's now or never!" Beverly takes her arm, but Eve looks catatonic. "Eve! We must go now!"

They sprint for the trees, through the sharp wild grass and weeds. Eve loses her footing and tumbles. Adam rides away and falls off Amanda's back. Amanda continues to gallop westerly. The Simerin lifts a shiny weapon, smiles an ugly, sinister smile, and shoots. Adam's body incinerates into ash. A puff of wind carries them across the field.

Beverly helps Eve to her feet, and they sprint the rest of the way into the woods. Out of the shadows, a man in a strange, gray suit runs to them. Beverly's eyes light up when she sees him. "Eric!" He takes her hand in the special way he does. "Are you alright? We saw the Sim heading in this direction."

"We're okay."

"There were three of you! Where's the male?" Beverly sadly shakes her head. Eve is unable to speak. This is not how it was supposed to end.

Eric places a hand on her shoulder. "He saved you, and he saved all of them, too." He points at a large group of people walking into a clearing toward a golden light.

Devil's Canyon

Victor fires from the rear of his transport. Another Simerin has joined the fight, so he has two Simerin on his tail. One explodes. Victor wishes he was in his fighter. This Sim is an excellent flyer, an even match, hanging with Victor's every move. Victor flies out of range, going west, over the Arizona desert, and can't shake him loose, and as if things couldn't get worse, more Simerin enter his radar, one coming in from the North, and one from the West. Victor hovers and waits. He flies straight up, and the two Simerin have a head-on collision. There's a huge explosion and debris rains down into Devil's Canyon.

One more to go and Victor's home free. He drops down and flies behind the Sim. Fires, but Victor gets outmaneuvered every time.

Victor scrunches his face. "Clever Sim!"

Another Simerin joins! Victor is trapped and takes hits. His shields have failed, and his craft is severely damaged. He must get back to the station without bringing this threat with him.

He locks fire on the craft in front of him. The clever Sim dips down into the deep gorge below. Victor loses sight of him.

Victor evaluates his dire situation. His shields and transport are compromised. Now he's unable to return fire. His only hope is to get out of this hot mess and return to the ship without jeopardizing the whole mission.

He flies low through the narrow canyon in the hopes he can escape by outmaneuvering them in Devil's Canyon. The canyon curves sharply to the left. Victor must turn the craft sideways and scrape through the small opening in the wall. The Sim thinks he can do the same but miss calculates. He crashes into the wall and explodes.

The emergency light on his panel flashes, signaling that the main station is under attack. The mission is over, and everyone must retreat.

"Victor, do you read me? You need to get back! Simerin are destroying the main hall of the station," His father reports. "I have your position. Return to the station now."

"I'm on my way." The canyon splits into two smaller ones. He takes the left fork. Victor thinks he made a break and can get back to the station, but a Sim fighter flies directly into his path. Victor pulls to the right to avoid the collision, but the canyon is too narrow. He ricochets off the canyon wall. SMASH! He sideswipes the Simerin fighter, spins out of control into the rocky gorge, and crash-lands. Victor's body lies amongst the rubble of his craft in the rocky, canyon floor.

It's too Late

Hundreds of other refugees swarm the landing dock, confused and nervous, as they unload onto the dock.

Beverly takes Eve by the hand, but Eve pulls away and walks to the other side of the dock. MinnEnKi's hand rests on Beverly's shoulder. "Try not to be too hard on yourself. She needs some space." MinnEnki and Beverly finally have a moment alone, and they embrace. "You did well, Beverly. I'm so proud of you."

"Adam saved our lives. We wouldn't have made it. Beverly swallows hard. "What about Anah? Where is she?"

"She and Yemo are okay. They're on a ship to NeuMonah."

"Is that where we're going?"

A red light flashes. "I need to get to the deck."

"What does the light mean?"

"It's an alert."

"What can I do?"

"Check everyone in and move them to the living quarters!"

Beverly raises her hand to get everyone's attention. "Excuse me, everyone. Please remain calm. There's food for everyone and beds. Please raise your hand if you can be a captain." Several volunteers raise their hands. "Great. Thank you!" Divide yourselves up into groups and give your names to your captain. Families, of course, stay together."

Beverly sorrowfully looks at Eve as she follows a group where hundreds of refugees wander around or rest on cots along the walls and floors. She passes out blankets and checks in with the captains' reports for any special needs or requests. Beverly approaches Eve and gives her a blanket. "Is there anything I can do or something you need?" Eve stares down at the floor. "I can come back later if you want."

"No...That's okay, you can stay. As long as you don't say that everything's going to be okay."

"Maybe I could sleep here on the cot next to you if you wouldn't mind."

Eve's eyes fill with tears. "I don't mind." She wipes away tears.

Beverly holds her hand as she weeps. "Everyone here is mourning. We can help each other get through this because that's all we have now is each other."

BANG! Beverly and Eve fall onto the floor. Women and children are screaming. AmanKi appears suddenly and tells everyone to stay calm, and that meals will be served shortly. We'll be on our way.

"I'll be right back," Beverly says to Eve and quickly gets up off the floor and approaches AmanKi. "What is going on? If you're going to hole us up in here, we have a right to know."

"We have things under control, but we've been discovered by Simerin, and we're surrounded by Simerin fire."

"Then why are we still here? Get us out of here!"

"It's Victor. He hasn't made it back."

CRASH! Everyone loses their balance and falls to the floor.

"It doesn't sound like things are under control!"

"We have some good fighters out there." BAM! People get shuffled around by another jolt and cry in fear.

"Someone should go get Victor!"

"It's too late."

"Maybe it's not!"

"I just lost communication with him and his transport. I'm telling MinnEnki to end this phase and complete the mission."

Beverly thinks of Anah. How will she explain this? She looks around at all the scared faces.

"You can tell her that Victor helped save most of the people here, that he's a hero. We can't let it all be for nothing." Beverly reaches for AmanKi's hand. She has a lump in her throat, unable to find her words. He returns to the bridge and disappears into the flashing, red warning light.

Last Sunset

"Whoa!" Alan spins around. "Did you see that? I saw something. Did anyone else?"

They walk closer to the edge of the canyon and stare down about a thousand feet. A lizard on a nearby rock bobs his head up and down. No wind, birds, or even a coyote calls out from the desert. "What did you see?" Chuchip asks.

"I'm not sure. It was a shadow of something flying, triangular. But it was so fast. Maybe I'm seeing things."

"Like a raven? They've been flying around."

"I want to go," says Hania. "Can we please go now?"

"Okay, tell me you saw that." Alan points.

"Was it a foo fighter?" Hania asks.

Willy puts his rifle strap over his shoulder. "That was an aircraft—an aircraft of foreign origin—flying illogically. Not one of ours."

"The first one was different. It didn't have any hard lines or edges. This one may be following the first one."

"Or chasing." Willy squints his eye in a way that makes him look more perceptive. "Something didn't seem friendly about it."

Willy rests Herc, his M4, against his chest and pauses. Their silhouette stands before a blazing sunset as the clouds change from bright pink to orange. He inhales deeply, like it may be his last. Chuchip holds Hania's hand. Hania looks at Alan, and takes his hand, too. Willy looks through the scope of his rifle but doesn't see anything out of the ordinary. He adjusts his eye patch. "Hania's right. We should leave. It's going to be dark soon." SLAM! A loud explosion catches them off guard. They take cover behind the van. KABOOM! Hania hugs his legs and covers his ears.

Willy peeks around the van and runs back to the edge of the canyon. "I think we got a soldier down, fellas." He looks at Alan. "Get to your car. Follow me!"

"What the hell for?"

"What does it look like? We're going down there!"

"Have you completely lost your mind?"

"Stay if you must. If you haven't noticed, we're in a war, and this could be the most important decision we make."

"Or our last!"

"That's right, but I'm not about to let them get away with this! This is still our planet, and we need to fight! We can't change the past. But we can change the future."

Alan tries to imagine his future and realizes that he can't. It's too grim to imagine under the circumstances. Living in the moment is his only choice. "Do you know the way down?"

Willy nods. "Follow me!"

He's on His Own

Victor's face is covered with dirt and sand. He attempts to blink his eyes open and focus. He's unable to move and tries to breathe. With blurred vision, he can tell he was thrown far from the wreckage. He begins to roll onto his side but experiences vertigo and has even more trouble standing. Blood drips from his head. Several ribs are broken in his chest and back. He tries to walk but there's a deep gash in his thigh muscle. Blood is pouring out. He quickly surveys the scattered remains of his transport, strewn across the canyon floor beyond repair. He removes his shirt and wraps it around his leg as a tourniquet. His face and arms are badly burned. Victor slowly stands but dizziness overtakes him. He loses his balance and falls onto his knee. A half mile south, a pillar of smoke rises out of the dark canyon into the light of the sunset. He's in no shape for a fight and hopes the Sim didn't survive the crash. He limps easterly, towards home. Is it too late to leave with the mission? He scans the sky for rescue. Something tells him that that ship has sailed, and he's on his own. He can't take a breath without experiencing excruciating pain and rests his back against a boulder. A cool desert breeze braises his body, signaling the end of the day, and with it, a warning. A pungent smell! Simerin!They find his ship and inspect it for survivors, sifting through scraps of metal and special alloy. One picks up Victor's scent and sees a trail of blood. The Sim notifies the others of his discovery. They laugh and discuss finding the monkey to finish him off and cook him for dinner to satisfy their hunger.

Victor looks for a place to hide. They aren't good fighters but one thing they are very good at is tracking. Victor knows he's in trouble. He could fight, but he's outnumbered five to one and has suffered too many injuries. He finds a crevice between the boulder he leans against and slides his body in between. There's a back opening at the rear of the crevice, but it's very narrow. He feels trapped. It's too late to get out.

"Hey, Ugly!" A strange voice yells from above. Victor doesn't recognize the voice. "Eat this!" POW! POW! POW! Bullets fly everywhere down into the canyon, even around Victor's head. A bullet ricochets off the boulder and lodges into Victor's shoulder. He's unable to move or crouch down because he's wedged between the rocks. After several minutes, the bullets stop flying.

"You can come out now," says the voice. "Hello?"

"Are you going to shoot me again?" Victor listens to the voices bicker amongst themselves about who might have made that mistake.

"Please, don't shoot!" Victor slides and scrapes his body while managing to come out and wonders how the heck he managed to get in. With bewilderment, he stares at the two young Hopi boys, the elder wearing the colorful eye patch, and the college kid wearing big black framed glasses and a tweed jacket. Yellow, Simerin blood and pieces of their flesh are splattered all over the canyon. "It's a pleasure to make your acquaintance," says Victor, then falls on his face and everything goes black.

We Can Pray

Willy feels for a pulse. "Is he dead?" asks Hania.

"He passed out, but his pulse is weak."

Alan looks into the eyes of the enemy. His body lays across some rocks. "How do we know if it's dead?" Alan asks frightfully. "Or doesn't wake up like it just had a nap or grow another head!"

Willy pokes him with the end of his M4. "He's dead. But we need to get out of here. They might have friends close by." Victor moans like he's trying to gain consciousness. "I have a stretcher in the van. He's coming with us." Willy looks at Hania and Chuchip. They run to the van and return with an old green, military stretcher. Together, they move Victor onto the stretcher and slide him into the van.

Alan adds pressure to Victor's gunshot wound and blood squirts out. "What should we do? Should we take him to a hospital?"

"Hospitals are a target. I'm sure those people are dead and have been abandoned by now. Besides, we're too far from one. We need to deal with this now." Willy takes out a scalpel and pours alcohol over it. "Okay, move that cloth." Willy pours alcohol all over Victor's shoulder. He takes his scalpel and digs out the bullet. Even more blood sprays out. "Apply Pressure!"

Alan presses the cloth onto the wound. "Where did you learn to do that?"

"Vietnam. Where else?" Willy removes the tourniquet from Victor's thigh and cleans the wound with water. "This is a mess. There's nothing I can do about that." It's too deep and torn. Help me dress it. Alan put fresh gauze over the gash. Willy wraps and pins it in place.

Chuchip rubs ointment on his burns. "Will he be okay?"

"It's up to him now. There's not much more we can do."

Hania slides forward to sit closer. "We can pray."

Willy softly converses with Chuchip and Hania in Hopi. They cover Victor with a Navajo blanket. Willy leads them out of the van and Alan follows them into the night. With a little moonlight leading the way, they arrive at a round Navajo abode.

Mi Shebeirach

Alan places his hand on the smooth, earthen wall. "What is this?" Alan asks.

"It's our hogan. It belonged to my father."

"I'm not sure what condition it is in. I haven't been here in a long time, since my father passed." Willy enters the circular, structure. The opening through the small doorframe is covered with a tapestry.

Alan ducks his head and steps through the doorway. "Did your father have ceremonies here?"

"It's for shelter from the hot sun, mostly. He Na'nilkaadi." Willy remembers Alan doesn't understand. "He was a shepherd... but he was famously known as a code talker during the Second World War and received a medal of honor from President Bush a few months before he died." They gently lower Victor onto the dirt floor. Chuchip holds the tapestry open to let in more moonlight. Willy strikes a match and lights an oil lantern, revealing the contents of the room: a wooden chair, a well-worn straw hat, a little clay pipe, and a leather pouch. A long cactus stick, with feathers hanging on the end, leans against the wall.

Willy places the pipe in the palm of his hand and packs the bowl with the sage tobacco from the leather pouch. He asks Chuchip to be his interpreter. "In darkness is when we pray, selfishly asking for light and forgiveness, hoping that Great Spirit hears our cries and gives mercy. When prayers turn on deaf ears, the wise remember to return to their roots and rediscover their true essence. In doing so, we realign our hearts with what is right...what is true. Only then do we realize the light is already there in each of us. Language, culture, and the color of our skin may separate us but we share this same light. That, in the end, is our power, and why we will never truly die but live forever."

He lights the bowl with a match. Chuchip and Hania sit close on either side of Victor. Willy sits in the chair behind Victor's head, and Alan sits by his feet. Chuchip begins to sing. Alan doesn't understand, but it sounds hauntingly sad and remorseful. Hania pours water over Victor's face, neck, hands, and feet then wipes them clean with a cloth. Willy lowers down and puffs smoke over Victor's face several times.

Alan thinks about Willy's words and whispers, "Who should I pray to?"

Willy passes him the pipe. "Pray to the God you know best."

Alan tries to remember the last time he was in the synagogue. The last time he had prayed was a happy time, celebrating his cousin's bar mitzvah. Alan looks over Victor's body. His hands and feet are large but in proportion to the rest of his extraordinary physique. He has lost a lot of blood and Alan is comforted that his blood is red, like his, unlike the creatures' yellow blood in the canyon. Alan notices something that seems curiously out of place. A woven leather necklace with a single turquoise bead is tied around his neck. Someone special gave it to him, he thinks. Someone who loves him and would be sad to lose him. In this little hogan, Alan suddenly feels a strong connection to everyone in the room. It even feels as if Victor's body is a part of his own. Alan puffs the smoke from the pipe. A Hebrew prayer, long forgotten, comes back to him all at once, and he prays to the only God he knows.

Mi Shebeirach ahvoteinu
M' Kor hab'racha L'imoteinu
Mi Shebeirach Imoteinu
M'Kor ha-brachah L'avoteinu
R'fuah Shleima Amen

Chuchip chants a prayer in Hopi and sings the words of his nation. Hania joins him. Willy puffs more smoke over Victor's head, face, and chest. They become weary, and their eyes heavy. Willy turns off the lantern, and they sleep in the cover of darkness not knowing if tomorrow will come again.

The Sun Still Rises

Light pours in through the crack of the doorway and the tapestry directly onto Alan's face. Alan reaches for his glasses and finds them in the bottom of his sleeping bag. With the sunrise, it brings a sense of relief. Maybe everything is back to normal, and the nightmare is over.

Alan springs to his feet. "He's gone!"

This wakes Chuchip and Hania. "Where did he go?"

Willy stirs, stretches, and rubs his eyes, as if he had two, and looks down at the stretcher where Victor's body should be. He blinks his eye several times and puts on his patch as if to see better.

They part the blanket like a curtain and gaze out into the brightness, dumbfounded. Victor sits on a rock, completely naked and still. His skin returned to a healthy gold, brown.

Alan whispers, "What's he doing?"

Willy steps outside of the hogan. "Hello?" Willy's voice carries away with an autumn wind, and Victor doesn't turn around. Willy scans Victor's body in disbelief. No burn marks, or bullet wounds, no gash on his thigh or broken bones. The only mark is a large tattoo of interlocking triangles on his back. Willy steps closer. "Do you understand me? Are you okay?"

"He looks more than okay," says Alan. "Look at him! Not even a scratch! He was at death's door last night."

Through the eyes of a raven, flying above Devil's Canyon, Victor scouts the area for Simerin. He sees a group of a dozen Simerin inspecting the deadly scene where he hid between the boulders.

The raven sweeps down and passes over their heads, Victor takes a deep breath and returns to his body. He climbs off the rock and approaches them. "I understand you. I appreciate your help with the Simerin and giving me a safe place to heal."

Victor's naked body makes Alan uncomfortable. He wonders if his prayer worked a miracle. Or perhaps, wonders Alan, he's not even human but A.I. Alan takes two awkward steps back. "Simerin? Are they the bad aliens?"

"Indeed, and they are not far away." Victor walks with big strides to his clothes and puts them on. "We need to go right away."

Chuchip picks up his backpack. "We don't know where we should go."

"I do." Victor walks several feet away. Willy and the boys

only stare, unsure of what they're witnessing. "Don't just stand there," Victor says.

"You speak English," says Willy. "That's a relief."

"And you understand Simerin."

"What are you talking about?"

"Those Simerin were talking about eating me, and you responded with, 'Eat this!' Then you shot them to pieces and everything, including me."

"Sorry about that. These guys are still learning."

"Nothing to forgive. I owe you my life. I'm pretty sure I would be burning over a Simerin fire right now if you decided to just go your own way. A bullet in the shoulder is a small price to pay."

"I didn't understand those uglies," Willy says.

Hania looks at Victor's arms and face, badly burned eight hours ago. "Where are your scars?"

"They healed."

"That's impossible."

"You helped when you poured water over me," he says with a wink.

"You weren't awake. How could you know that?"

"I saw it. I was in the room. My body was in bad shape."

"You left your body?"

"Yes. Almost for good."

"Are you glad that you didn't?"

"I'm glad to be here, and there's much work to do."

After they hike to the vehicles, Alan says. "Um... I have a question. Where are we going?"

"Abiquiu." Victor points to Alan's Subaru. "I'll ride with you. Willy, you don't mind following, do you? Let's take the pass through the mountains. If we get separated, our meeting place is the lake. I'll wait for you there. If you haven't noticed, the temperature is dropping, and those clouds will bring snow in the higher elevations. So, let us make hast." They look at the dark clouds gathering over the mountains to the north, and a cold wind blows across their faces.

Willy stows away his stretcher in the van. "What's at the lake?"

"I'll explain when we get there." Victor climbs into the Subaru.

Sorry Improvisations

The image of an AK-47 sitting on the back seat of the Subaru is something Alan wouldn't have imagined in a million years. Soldiering isn't for him. He's only watched one war movie in his life and that was in high school in history class. It made him feel less human and he hated that. Science is what he was born to do. But when your freedom to live is taken, the only thing left to do is fight. This is a side of him that he will cultivate. The instinct to survive is coded in his DNA.

With Alan and Victor leading the way, they caravan up the dusty road and merge onto the interstate.

Alan glances at Victor. "I saw you fly by, in the canyon, when they were after you." Victor nods. "What exactly is going on?"

"Simerin are invading Earth." Victor looks out through the window.

"I always knew there was intelligent life beside us. Mathematically, it's not only plausible but guaranteed." Alan glances in the review mirror to make sure Willy is close behind and slows down. "These Simerin, they killed everyone. I mean, it's like they're exterminating us, like ants."

"That's what they're doing."

"Why is this happening?"

"They don't create life. They destroy it. That's what gives them a sense of power and control."

"If they don't create life, how do they even exist?"

"Cloning. This wasn't always so, but since they're no longer connected to life force, they try to hold on to power by destroying it."

"So, we should destroy them before they destroy life."

"They give us no choice."

Alan steals another glance and marvels at Victor's perfectly healed body.

Victor smiles from the side and puts his hand on Alan's shoulder. "I appreciate your words. The prayer you spoke."

Alan raises his eyebrow and adjusts his glasses. He looks to the Sandia mountains and wonders about his future. It feels as if there's little time left. Everything has changed in an instant. He doesn't even have a girlfriend. He was popular only because he helped other students with their assignments. Anah was the first girl, besides his mother, that he had longer than a five-minute conversation with. He never imagined someone as beautiful and smart as Anah would actually be interested in him.

Victor stares at him. "Uhh... can I help you with something?"

Victor puts his hand on the back of Alan's headrest. "Tell me about this girl?"

"Uhh... girl?"

"You met at school... she's in the same physics class as you."

"Okay... how do you know this?"

"Sorry. You think loudly."

"You can read minds?"

Victor looks out the window. Alan exits the interstate and takes a left towards Jemez Pueblo. Snow falls on the windshield. "That's a bit rude, don't you think? You should have warned me. I could be thinking about anything, you know, private things."

"It would be like you saying, Oh, by the way, if you don't mind, I'm going to breathe, so don't be offended."

"I guess I shouldn't be surprised. If you can leave your body and fly in a bird. So, what else can you do?"

"Crash my transport."

"Well, besides that."

"I should be the one asking questions."

"Like what?"

"Like how do you know Anah?"

"Hold on. How do you know Anah? Wait! Don't tell me. She's one of you! That's it! And so is her cousin, or boyfriend, whoever he is."

"Yemo is her brother."

"So, Anah's mother lied to me."

"I'm sure it was for a good reason. She has no idea where Anah is or why she left."

"Where did she go?"

"NeuMonah."

"Is that where you're from?"

"Yes. We come from the star system of Aldebaran. Earth is one of our colonies." Victor chuckles.

"What's so funny?"

"I'm sorry. I'm not making fun of you. It's just funny that you have a crush on Anah."

"You think she's out of my league?"

Victor chuckles again at the irony as he tries to see out the window through large, heavy snowflakes. "Look out!"

Alan slams on his brakes, slides, and spins off the road to avoid hitting a herd of cattle. Willy must slam his brakes to avoid crashing into the Subaru.

"Oh shit. Now what?"

"Just drive back onto the road. You're fine. Look. The cattle are moving."

Alan gets back on track and drives slower with his window wipers on full speed as they approach the Jemez Pueblo. He looks for signs of life. "The Hopi village was also abandoned. Hard to tell if anyone's there with this storm. Maybe they're all hunkered down." The houses and cars are buried under a thick blanket of snow already.

"The Hopis were rescued with the Chantallah," Victor says.

"Chantallah?"

"It means the chosen."

"You picked certain people to save?"

"They are genetically programmed to leave Earth. It can happen anytime, in this life or another. It doesn't usually happen with a mass migration."

"I guess I wasn't a part of that special group," says Alan, straining to see through the heavy snowfall.

"Your purpose is unfolding now. You saved my life and Willy and those two boys."

"I didn't do anything. I would be dead if it wasn't for them."

"It started when your car failed to start. Willy picked you up and then you found the boys. If you weren't there, they would be dead. I would be dead. We'd all be dead."

"So, you can read minds and see past events?"

"Again, your thoughts are loud."

A strong wind gust pushes the car and sudden whiteout conditions. Alan's window wipers can't keep up. "I can't see!"

"Just stop the car."

Alan looks back for Willy. "I can't see shit! Where's Willy? He's not behind us." THUMP.

"You drove off the road."

Alan puts it in reverse and gets stuck. He tries to move forward and backward. "Now what?"

Willy knocks on the window. "You okay?"

"We're fine," says Victor.

"The van can't drive through this."

Victor opens his door against the heavy wind and snow

blows into the car. "We need to find shelter and wait out this storm. Pack what you can carry."

"Hurry! Those foo-fighters might be near," Chuchip calls out from the top of the ditch.

Everyone stuffs food and water into backpacks, grabs a rifle, and gathers around the van.

"What do you mean by, 'Foo Fighters?'" Victor asks.

Willy strains his voice to be heard over the storm. "Some kind of crazy, high-tech weaponry... glowing balls in the sky that created an intense high pitch sound. People lost their minds and started killing themselves. If they didn't, they ran out into the streets to escape the sound only to get fired upon."

"The Air Force finally took them out with missiles," Alan continues.

"I guess we'll just have to see if they have more of these strange weapons," says Victor over the storm. "This is already a huge risk driving over this mountain."

Willy shields his face from the snow. "This is your idea, not mine."

"I thought we could get ahead of the storm. The village is six miles back. We'll wait out the storm there."

Without protest, they get into the van and attempt to turn around. The van gets stuck and Willy presses on the gas pedal hard, but the front tires spin endlessly without any traction.

Victor lets out a deep sigh. "Get your warmest clothes on. We must walk." Hania puts on the red hat that he and his brother found in the Arizona desert hunting for snakes. "That's it? Don't you have a coat?"

Chuchip crosses his arms. "Sorry if we didn't pack a suitcase with our ski clothes."

"What about you? You're not wearing a coat?" Hania looks at the rather thin, torn layer of Victor's spacesuit.

"I don't need to. This material keeps me warm," Victor says taking off his clothes.

Alan looks away. "He's getting naked again."

Victor gives Hania his space suit. "Put this on. It will protect you from the wind."

"I have more clothes, but I have to go back to my car," says Alan.

Willy opens the van door. "What are you waiting for?" Alan runs to the Subaru and retrieves a duffle bag.

Willy gathers up blankets and gives one to Victor. "Here. Wrap these around you, at least."

Alan jumps back into the van, brushes the snow off and zips open his duffle. A winter hat and ski gloves for Chuchip and wool socks as gloves for Hania's hands. "What will you wear?" Hania asks Alan.

"I have this coat with a hood and extra clothes," he says, sliding wool socks over his hands and up his arms. "Chuchip, you can wear my ski pants. It looks like they'll fit."

Willy puts on his army jacket and wraps a wool blanket around him. He picks up his rifle and looks at the gang. "If the foo fighters don't kill us, this storm will, and I should mention, if we even make it to the village, they don't allow weapons. Maybe under the circumstances, it will be okay." Victor eyes the crossbow mounted on the inside wall of the van and looks at Willy for permission. Willy nods with approval.

Blue Flash

Wind and snow sting their eyes. Victor's blanket blows off his naked body. Under normal circumstances, he can handle freezing temperatures for long periods by using his breath in a certain way. However, he's not wearing any clothing, and the wind chill is minus ten. He picks up his blanket and wraps it tighter, using the crossbow to hold it in place. He concentrates on his breathing. He didn't get this far to die on this mountain of exposure.

Hania has a hard time walking. It's deeper than expected, and it comes up to his thighs. Their tire tracks are already covered, and it's nearly impossible to see.

Victor knows that they will freeze if they continue moving so slowly. He picks Hania up onto his back and wraps him inside the blanket.

"You'll help keep me warm," Victor says.

Hania welcomes the added warmth and doesn't mind.

Alan stops to catch his breath even though the cold air burns his lungs. His glasses aren't doing him any good, so he puts them in his coat pocket. "I think we should go back to the van!" He yells over the wind.

Willy's bright eye patch stands out against the white background. "It's too late to turn around!"

Chuchip stops and doesn't move.

"What's wrong?" Willy asks.

"I hear a strange noise."

"What noise?"

"I hear it," says Victor. "It sounds like scraping metal."

"Where is it coming from?" Alan says.

Chuchip looks up to the sky, but all he can see is snow. "It's coming from up there."

"Get into those trees!" Victor grabs Alan by the arm, and they scurry away into the pines.

Alan bends over, trying to recover his breath. "What are we doing?"

Victor sets Hania down next to a large ponderosa. "We're hiding."

Hania pulls his hat down over his ears. "Is it foo fighters?"

"I don't know," says Victor. "Is that what they sound like?"

"No. You wouldn't be able to stand it," says Alan. "I mean, this sound is creepy, but it's not like someone's drilling into your skull."

Victor sets the crossbow against the tree. The sound of scraping metal in the sky grows louder. A blue flash lights up the sky.

"Get down!" Victor pushes them into the snow and covers their bodies with the blanket, and they huddle under the pines. The snow completely covers them, and they disappear. The scraping metal sound is directly above them. The blue light flashes through the pines.

"Keep your eyes closed," Victor holds everyone close. "Do not open them until I say so!"

Hania's body trembles, stricken with fear. Victor tells him to think of something that makes him feel safe. Hania thinks of his father who would play a song on his flute at bedtime. It would put him into a dreamy slumber and his mind at ease. He hears the song his father plays and hums the tune.

"I think it's gone," Alan whispers.

Victor and Willy slowly stand. The snow breaks away from the blankets. Cautiously, Victor blinks his eyes open. "Okay. You can open your eyes."

Hania is still crouched down, holding his head, and humming the tune. Willy puts his hand on his back, "Hania. It's okay now."

One Foot at a Time

The forest provides some shelter from the wind, but every so often a branch cracks and snaps under the weight of the snow.

Victor lifts his nose to the air and recognizes the faint smell of smoke.

Chuchip smells it, too. "There's smoke coming from over there," he points. Under a thick canopy of snow-covered branches, they spy a small cabin in the distance. "Come on!"

This gives the gang hope and renewed energy. They quicken their pace.

A sudden wind gust blows the branches and dumps snow on top of Willy. He loses his footing, slips, and falls into a ravine they walk along, and cartwheels down to the bottom.

Luckily, the snow breaks his fall, and he doesn't land hard on the rocks. Victor slides down on his rear after him, and the boys follow down, one by one. Willy tries to recover but falls again and lands in a creek meandering under the snow. That's when Victor realizes—Willy's not well.

Victor reaches out his hand. "I can carry you the rest of the way. We're almost there."

Willy doesn't want to be the weak link in the group. He grabs Victor's arm and puts his weight on his rifle and struggles to his feet. "I'm fine."

Alan retrieves Willy's blanket—it snagged on a dead cedar branch— shakes it dry, and wraps it around Willy.

"You don't look fine," says Chuchip. "Can you walk the rest of the way?"

"Yes. But I don't want to slow us down."

Victor surveys the area. "We can take a shortcut. We must cross the creek and climb up that steep, rocky ridge. Or, if you prefer, the longer easier route." Victor hears the unanimous vote in his head. "The shortcut it is."

Chuchip points. "Look!" There's a log crossing further up the ravine, covered in a couple of feet of snow.

Victor leads the way. "I'll clear the snow. Just wait for me to cross first. And don't look down!" Victor steps closely, one foot at a time, shuffling through the snow to clear the way. He looks back to the gang when he finally reaches the other side. He cups his hands and yells, "Hania, you're next."

Hania crosses with ease. Chuchip follows, joins his brother on the other side, and gives him a fist bump. Alan steps onto the log but looks down at the rocks and the moving water below. He feels dizzy and steps back from the log.

"Don't look down! Focus a few feet in front of you!" Victor says.

Alan starts again and focuses a few feet in front of him, calculating where to place his feet. Halfway, his focus begins to falter, and he's afraid to take another step.

Victor walks out to meet him. "It's okay. Just stay calm. Take a deep breath and follow me." Together they walk the rest of the way across. Chuchip and Hania fist bump Alan.

Willy stands before the log bridge without expression. His face, pale. He's unable to focus and see properly. He leans against a tree to brace himself. Victor walks back across.

"Hold on," Victor says, as he lifts Willy onto his back.

"This video would totally go viral." Alan rubs his wool socks together. "Naked man from another planet carries one-eyed Indian across a ravine in a blizzard."

"Hey look!" Hania announces. "That tree up at the top has a rope tied to it. We're on a trail. There's a rope somewhere around here." He kicks away the snow. "Here it is! I found it!" Shaking it loose from the ground, he pulls it out from under the snow.

Victor has six more feet to go before they reach the other side. He pauses and regains his balance but leans too far to the left and slips, leans too far to the right, and slips again. Hania drops the rope, and all three boys catch their breath and watch in horror. He finds his balance for a second and in three quick leaps reaches the other side.

Alan pushes his glasses up and blinks several times. "That was the craziest thing I ever saw."

Hania secures his rifle on his back and picks up the rope. "This should be easy then." He gives the rope a couple of test tugs.

Listless and sick, Victor sets Willy down. "You okay?"

Willy gives them the thumbs up.

"Go ahead, Hania. Same order." Victor bends down and gives Willy a pat on the shoulder. "We're almost there." He wraps the blanket around Willy's head and shoulders. "You got this, soldier."

After the boys scale the side of the ravine, Victor wraps the rope under Willy's arms and legs and climbs to the top. Willy looks up and gives them a thumbs-up. Victor and the gang slowly pull Willy on the other end. Willy manages to use his legs to help. A branch snaps and Willy slips and bangs into the side of the ravine. Finally, they heave him to the surface and free him from the rope. Victor hoists him up onto his back and carries him. Someone has been expecting their arrival, Victor knows. In a hundred yards, they will learn who.

NeuMonah

I step off the platform. A welcoming breeze greets us on the dock. My blue scarf blows off my shoulders, so I give it an extra wrap around my neck. A sun sets over a low horizon, and I shield my eyes from the light with a second sun right above it. Gentle rolling hills and forests are to the north. So far, besides having two suns, nothing seems too out of the ordinary on NeuMonah. The grass is green and the sky is blue. The sweet scent of honey carries on the breeze and blows through my hair. The valley to the east grows wild grasses and flowers teaming with insects and snow-white, deer-like, animals graze. One lifts his head, and with a whistle sound from his nose, informs the others of the disturbance.

I turn to Yemo and laugh. "This is not what I expected."

"You expected a welcome party?" Yemo swings a canvas bag over his head.

"Sign of inhabitants, maybe."

"Don't worry. They know we're here."

"Should I be worried?" Yemo laughs. I give my brother a poke with my elbow. "What's so funny?"

"You worry too much."

Crew members dock their pods and scatter about, happy to have feet on the ground. After nearly two Earth years of space travel, they return to their homes.

Something odd catches my attention. The crew have an iridescent glow and appear less solid, looking almost transparent at times, especially when they make sudden, swift moves. I rotate my arm around in the air and observe the same phenomena. This gives me a light, euphoric feeling.

Smiling, Yemo says, "Welcome to NeuMonah."

"What is this about?"

"Our vibration is adjusting to that of the planet."

"I feel light, like I'm on a cloud. Maybe I died and went to heaven."

"You are more alive than you've ever been," says Paki walking up from behind. A woman with two young children, a boy, and a girl, approach us. She cries tears of joy when she sees Paki. She's elegant, tall, with flawless, dark skin and a beautiful, infectious smile.

The kids run to him, screaming, "Papa!"

Paki hugs the boy. "Davu!" He picks up his daughter and kisses her forehead. "Oni!" Paki wraps his free arm around his wife, and they meld together as one.

My eyes well up with tears. *"How long has it been since they've seen him?"* I ask telepathically to Yemo.

The woman turns and looks directly at me. "27 moons," she answers.

"My apologies." My cheeks flush. "I didn't know that you can—"

"Of course. It's okay."

Paki steps aside. "Anah meet my family. My wife, Amari. My son and daughter, Davu, and Oni."

I kneel to look at the children. "It's very nice to meet you."

Amari bows. "Nahmah."

"Nahmah."

"You're most welcome to stay with us until you have a place of your own."

"That's very kind of you. I didn't think about where I was going to stay."

"Yemo," Amari gives him a warm hug. "Thank you for returning my husband to us safe and sound!"

"I don't think we'd be here if it wasn't for him."

"Come and join us. I prepared a meal. I'm anxious to learn about your journey and wish to get acquainted with Anah." Amari speaks with an accent, different from Paki. She looks over my lean body. "It looks like you could use a home-cooked meal. Vegetables are fresh from the garden."

Yemo and I accept the invitation and follow Paki and his family to their home. Similarly, like Victor's cob house, it's sculpted right out of the ground with several domes and circular windows. The outside wall is painted in an intricate blue and white design that wraps around the front of the house in a spiral. There's a large, old tree in a private courtyard.

I marvel at the mural. "Wow! This is beautiful."

"Paki and I made it. It reminds us of our roots. My African roots and his Jamaican."

"Do you wish to go back?"

"This is our home now."

Amari serves a variety of colorful, homegrown vegetables and fresh fruit from the market that she wants to visit with me in the morning.

"Thank you for making my very first meal on NeuMonah. It's delicious."

Davu and Oni fall asleep on Paki's lap. The candles glow onto their little faces. Amari gently picks up Davu and whispers, "You're very welcome. Time to get the children tucked in." Paku carries Oni and follows his wife out of the courtyard and into the house.

Yemo entertains himself with the flame of the candle. I clear some plates. *Perhaps we've stayed long enough. We should give them their privacy.*" Amari is in the other room and tele-pathically asks me to stay a little while longer.

"*Oh, sure. I didn't want to impose.*"

She returns to the courtyard. "You're not an imposition, Anah."

An evening bird coos in the big, white tree. Branches arch downward, almost touching the ground, before curving upwards again. An enormous moon, twice the size of Earth's, highlights the curving, twisting branches. Another smaller moon lies lower on the horizon, casting a burnt orange color over the landscape.

"I'm grateful that you and the others made it back." Amari places her hand on top of Paki's. "It was very fortunate. Others, however, did not. Some of our dear friends have perished. It's a time to rejoice but also a time to mourn." Her large, almond-shaped, brown eyes reflect the candlelight. "Why? What's happening?"

Yemo leans on the table. "Simerin orchestrated, surprisingly, a well-planned attack to take over the colony. Paki was able to separate from the main station before it was destroyed."

"AmanKi... is he alive?"

"AmanKi, and our father, lead the Chantallah mission. We have no word if they succeeded."

"If so, the refugees will come here?"

"Yes."

Amari interlaces her fingers. "Then there's much work to be done. We should prepare for their arrival. Do you have any idea when that could be?"

Yemo taps his fingers on the table. "It depends on many circumstances." He speaks in Monahdah.

My thoughts drift to Victor. I may see him soon, but my gut doesn't share the same feeling. I wrap my scarf across my neck with the fresh evening air. "Amari, how do you know AmanKi?"

"He's my brother-in-law."

"So that means..."

"My sister is Victor's mother."

"Victor told me she died in a civil war."

"She was a refugee, as was I. She starved while breastfeeding orphans. Paki and I woke up on a ship that brought us here, but my sister was already..." Amari catches her breath. "She died moments before we were rescued."

"I'm sorry. I didn't mean to... It's none of my business." This information certainly helps me understand Victor's painful past, and the unspoken hostility he has toward his father. "What's her name?"

"Akhet. We were twins."

I admire Amari's beauty, her defined lips and high cheekbones. Her complexion glows with peach undertones. I wonder if they were identical twins. Maybe I'm looking at a spitting image of Victor's mother.

Amari smiles softly. "Yes, identical twins."

The smaller moon is almost directly above us, and the tree is silent from the bird's cooing. "I would like to help you prepare for the Chantallah."

Amari stands and smooths out her white linen dress.

"Thank you, Anah. It will take many hands." She smiles, and I feel her kind heart. "You're welcome to stay here if you want."

"I'm sure Yemo is getting tired of me, but I'll stay with him tonight in our father's home, thank you."

Paki laughs, "They'll just take it out on each other in the Kalari tomorrow. Yemo gets to fight with weapons, but Anah's only defense is a scarf."

Amari puts her hands on her hips "That doesn't seem fair."

In one swift move, I remove my scarf, wrap it around Yemo's arm, and pin it behind his back. "Time to go, brother."

"Wow! It looks like a scarf is all she needs," laughs Amari.

I wrap the scarf around my head. "Goodnight. I'll see you tomorrow at the market."

"See you tomorrow."

The moon's light shines our way home. I should be tired, but I've never felt so alive. "I feel energized, Yemo. Like I can do anything."

"NeuMonah Da Florah Ahman Vedah."

"I think you're saying that the planet is enlightened."

"A healthy planet and healthy people lead to a healthy society. It's all connected. Also, we were on the ship for many moons. You're feeling the relief that feet on the ground can bring. I feel it too."

I follow Yemo through winding pathways. We pass a cluster of dome dwellings. I feel guilt walking along the peaceful neighborhoods of NeuMonah, when I imagine the terror Simerin has caused on Earth, I feel it. Simerin infested the planet. Perhaps all is lost. The question remains in my mind. Is Earth worth saving?

"All may not be lost," Yemo responds. "We will win Earth back." We turn to walk up a long flight of stone steps. Two young boys giggle when they see me. "When we do win, we'll start over."

"Start over how?"

"Start over with the correct mentality and create a new world. We won't let Simerin rape Earth, so why should we continue to let anyone else? A planet is a gift, not a privilege."

We reach the top of another flight of stairs. I notice a quality in Yemo that I haven't seen before. He's relaxed and less guarded.

"Here we are—Home."

A cluster of dome structures look down on the city. The center entrance is a large atrium that opens to a space full of exotic plants, flowers, and a natural water feature in the middle.

I put my hand through the atrium bubble. "What is this?"

"It's a barrier that controls the climate for the plants. You'll see it tomorrow at the market."

"I didn't know you had such a green thumb." He looks bewilderedly at his hands. I bend down and closely examine little twinkling lights. "I mean gardening, silly." Small, pink flowers with star-shaped faces open their peddles towards the moonlight.

"This is Meirlies. I don't know about plants."

I use my index finger and poke the iridescent, pink glow of the flower.

"Those flowers," Yemo says bending down, "are Chandah-mas. They bloom only when the moon is full."

"Then you do know something about plants. I can't wait to explore more when Mom, Victor, and Meirlies get here."

"What about me?"

I give him a playful shove. "Of course. All of us together as a family. Like what Paki has."

"I don't know if I'll ever have a life like Paki."

"Why do you think that?"

"I'm a keeper, not a breeder. I won't always be around. Just like Meirlies isn't here now, or Victor, and the other Keepers."

"Amari and Paki are making it work." He shrugs his shoulders. I feel the weight of his concern. It's deeper than I realized. It's hard to forget that most people on Earth are now dead, and he thinks Sophia must be among them.

"You miss Sophia."

"I don't know this word, 'miss.' But I do like the way I feel when I'm with her, and when I think about her."

I hug Yemo. "Then you miss her."

"I hope you're comfortable here. This is your home now. Tomorrow..." He swirls his hand around in the fountain.

"What about tomorrow?"

"Tomorrow is a big day," he grins.

"Another party?"

"It's going to be the festival of all festivals."

"Really? I only saw two little kids so far. No big welcome parties here."

Yemo walks into a living room area and sits in a cove of cushions and pillows. "They are giving you space and time to get settled. They knew you'd appreciate that."

"And how did they, whoever they are, know that?"

"I told them."

"I see. Well, I'm supposed to go with Amari to the market tomorrow."

"Right. That's the plan."

"Why are you telling me this now?"

"It's supposed to be a surprise, but I learned, from the last time, that you hate surprises."

I laugh and throw a pillow at him. "So why make it a surprise at all?"

"I don't know."

I wrap my arms around a soft, linen pillow. "Well, I guess we shouldn't spoil the surprise. It's ridiculous, anyway. You can't have a Monahdah surprise when you can read minds."

"That's why it's fun." Yemo looks at me as if he's seeing me for the first time. "Why are you looking at me like that?"

"I can't believe I have a sister, and here you are in my house."

"It is hard to believe. I'm a part of all this and was kept away for so long."

"The important thing is you are here now."

"You're right. I shouldn't dwell on the past, especially when we need to talk about what we're going to do about the present situation with the Simerin. And what about Sahn—

that traitor? He's Monahdah, and he tried to kill us. That means even Monahdah can be misguided."

Yemo leans back and crosses his arms. "He won't get away with it, and he can't hide forever. We will know more when Meirlies returns with the Chantallah."

"You mean if — not when."

Yemo acknowledges with a sigh. He gazes upward as if he's looking for a sign. "In the meantime, we train. We meet in the Kalari after the celebration."

You're Here

They step onto a little porch. Victor places Willy on a wooden bench. Alan clears the snow away from the window, cups his hands, and sees only darkness. "It doesn't look like anyone's here."

Chuchip looks under the wood bench at two pairs of worn, muddy, hiking boots. "Someone lives here."

Victor inhales, and his nostrils flare. "The smoke led us here. I think someone was trying to guide us."

Alan knocks on the door. "Hello? Anyone here? We need some help. Can we come in?"

The door creaks open. A teenage girl stands in the doorway. "You're here," she says with a smile on her face.

Victor helps Willy to his feet. "May we come in? We require shelter."

She opens the door wider and steps aside. "I've been

expecting you. Put your weapons down by the door. I have dry clothes and blankets warming by the wood stove."

Alan bangs into a table. "Can we turn the lights on? It's black as ink in here."

She strikes a match, lights a gas lantern, and turns down the flame to a soft glow. The light shines into her eyes, and it startles the boys unexpectedly. "I'm sorry to startle you," she says. "I'm blind."

Victor looks into her white cloudy eyes. "How did you know we were coming?"

"I saw it in my mind. I've seen the images so many times, and now I can't believe you're here." She continues excitedly, "I know what you look like, what you're wearing, your voices, your names."

The soft glow of the oil lamp illuminates the room, and the gang notices the five neatly folded piles of clothes on a cot next to the wood stove. She picks up a pile and gives it to Chuchip. "These are for Willy. You must remove his wet clothes immediately and put him here by the stove. I have water to soak his feet. These are for you and your brother. Alan, these are for you." She picks up the last remaining pile. "I apologize, Victor. These are the best I could do. They were too short, so I sewed an extra bit on the hem."

Victor holds up his new clothes. "This is very generous of you...what's your name?"

"Emily."

"Thank you, Emily."

Victor glances around the room. On the table is a bottle

of whiskey, some white paper, a freshly sharpened meat cutter, antiseptic, and rolls of gauze. He furrows his brow and squints at the closed door. Victor opens the door and shines the lantern into the room. A man lies on a bed with his dark, hard-toiled hands neatly folded on his stomach. His eye sockets are black and burned hallow.

Emily steps into the room. "The flashing light took my father. The same light that you hid from."

"I'm very sorry. We should move his body outside. Do you need more time with him?"

Emily wipes away her tears. "I've said my goodbyes."

Alan and Hania step into the dimly lit room holding the meat cutter and antiseptic. "What are these for? Uh...who's that? Oh my God! What happened to him?" Victor wraps the body in the blanket. "Emily's father was killed by the blue flash."

Outside the room, next to the wood stove, Chuchip removes Willy's boots and Willy yells, "Leave me alone! I'm fine!"

Chuchip says something in Hopi and carefully pulls the boot off. The rest of the gang joins them. Chuchip slowly peels away Willy's soaking wet sock. His foot is swollen and blistered. Some toes are almost black.

"Holy...!" Alan exclaims. "Frostbite!"

Emily places her hand on Victor's arm. "My father can wait. You must do this now."

Victor picks up the bottle of whiskey and gives it to Willy. "We can save your foot." Willy drinks the whiskey like water and nods. Victor rubs his hands together vigorously for several seconds then places his hands on Willy's foot. Generating a tingling sensation, heat travels into his foot and up his leg. The infection recedes. Except for three black toes, the color of his foot returns to normal and the swelling goes down. Victor takes the butcher knife from Alan. SLAM! Three toes drop onto the wood floor, save the big toe and the next one. Flawlessly working together, Alan drenches a cloth with the antiseptic and Hania applies it to Willy's foot. Chuchip quickly wraps the foot with gauze. Emily delivers painkillers, and he swallows them down with another drink of whiskey.

"Thank you," mumbles Willy. His eyes close. "I feel better already." His body shivers, and he lies down on the cot. Hania places a warm cloth on his head and covers him with a blanket.

Victor pulls Emily aside, and whispers, "Is this the end of your vision?"

She sits down at the table and runs her fingers across the brail on the white paper. "The storm will break in three days. Then we disembark to the lake."

"We?" Alan says, eavesdropping.

"That's where things get blurry," she says.

Victor can hear her thoughts as she tries to place the pieces of the puzzle. He sees, in a brief flash, Anah in her vision. This confuses him. Anah is surrounded in darkness and the vision is difficult to see.

"What's clear, though," she explains, "is I go with you. Until then, we have three days. I made plenty of stew, and you can rest. We're going to need it." She puts on a mitten, lifts the lid to the pot on the stove, and stirs the hot, steamy stew. Hania and Chuchip smell the stew and feel very hungry. "Victor, you must eat, also. You will be without your red stone for a long time."

"Thank you. But we should move your father if you don't mind."

"I tried to warn him. In the end, the warnings weren't enough. He said I was just having a silly dream."

While Willy recuperates on the cot, the gang carries the body through the woods, passing a pile of recently split wood, and a stable where two horses and a mule are sheltered. After they dig through two feet of snow they find ground and take turns digging. With the last light of day and as darkness settles around them, they finish. With the snow and wind at their backs, they return to the cabin.

Steam rises from the soup. Hania and Chuchip wash up before they sit at the table. Emily shows them how to use the water pump and pumps water into a tub on the floor.

Spoons clanging and happy slurping prompts Willy to lift his head and sit up on the edge of the cot. Emily brings him some stew, and he cradles the warm bowl in his hands.

"Thank you." The warm stew feels good in his empty stomach. "I'm very sorry for your loss. Do you live here?"

"My father and I stay here in the summers, mostly, and we'd come for about a week in the fall. My parents, and with a little help from our mule, Lucky, built this place before I was born. When we heard the emergency broadcast, we thought we would be safe here. This place was always our escape plan."

Alan scrapes the bottom of his bowl with a piece of bread.

"My parents have a cabin upstate New York. I told them to go there, but I don't think it's safe anywhere."

Victor walks over to the window and looks through the parted curtains. "You don't have a vehicle?"

"We have the mule and two horses. There's no way to drive up here. We park down below where the road ends and hike. It's a good day hike on foot or with the horses, about three hours."

"We appreciate you taking us in," says Victor.

"Thank you for helping me with my father." Emily dries a bowl and sets it on the drying rack.

With full stomachs and warm beds, Chuchip and Hania fall into a deep sleep on cots pushed together. Hania has nightmares, so Chuchip wants to be close to his brother. Alan sleeps on a leather sofa lined with sheep skins. Willy and Victor take Emily's father's bed, and Emily sleeps up in her loft.

Willy and Victor lie side by side, listening to the howling wind and the snow blowing against the window. Tree branches in the near distance break under the weight of the snow and wind. Willy removes his eye patch and sets it on the nightstand next to the gas lantern. "Are you okay with this?" He slurs his words from the whiskey and painkillers.

"With what? You and me sharing the same bed?" Victor puffs.

"I'm talking about sleeping in the same bed that a dead man was in a few hours ago. His spirit is probably still hanging around."

"Oh, sure. Don't worry about it. Get some rest, Willy."

After a few moments, Willy says, "Thank you for what you did...getting me over that bridge. I would have died out there or from the gangrene."

"Don't mention it. Yesterday, you did the same for me. I would have been mauled by Simerin without your help."

"I wonder how many more yesterdays we have left?" Willy slurs.

"Just get some rest. According to Emily, we have more days ahead."

"We have to fight every day until our breath... last breath."

"I think you had too much of that whiskey, Willy."

"I'll fight for us. But mostly for Mother."

Victor folds his hands on his chest. "The planet?"

"She's our home, our gift, and we can't leave her to be destroyed by these uglies." Willy rolls onto his side, farts, and begins to snore.

Victor is unable to rest, so he wanders into the living room. He looks at the boys sleeping. Their faces are soft and restful, and this makes him sad. They have no idea what lies ahead. The odds are against them. Someone could die if not all of them.

He quietly rocks back and forth in the chair. "I won't let that happen. What kind of Keeper am I if I don't know how to keep them safe? I will get them through this even if it's my last breath." He continues to ruminate, "I made the right decision not to go back to the ship. More Simerin would have followed me. Meirlies should safely reach NeuMonah, soon to join Anah and Yemo." He softly smiles, thinking of Anah. Soon she will be reunited with Beverly. This appeases his mind, knowing they are safe.

Feeling the warmth of the red, glowing coals burning, he closes his eyes wishing he had his Mon. If his body withstands more duress, it will take longer to heal himself and harder to heal others, like Willy's leg.

BANG! BANG! BANG! He jolts awake. Someone knocks loudly at the door. He opens the door and snow blows into the cabin. A woman removes her head cover, and her hair blows across her face. Anah!

Victor opens his eyes and looks around the room. He's still in the rocking chair. The front door is closed. Everyone's asleep.

"Are you dreaming of her?" He spins around to see Emily standing behind him.

"I'm sorry." She wraps a blanket around her shoulders and whispers, "I didn't mean to startle you. I'm unable to sleep."

"Me, too. I imagine with a cabin full of strangers it would be uncomfortable."

"You don't feel like strangers to me."

"How did you know I was dreaming of her?"

"I didn't. That's why I asked."

"Well, you guessed right. It felt very real."

"Maybe it wasn't a dream but a vision."

Victor guides her to a chair to sit. "Have you seen Anah in your visions?"

"Yes."

"Have you had more visions?"

"They've been stronger since you all got here. It can happen anytime. I could be cooking or eating. I never know when."

"What do you see—when you have visions of Anah?"

"It's usually a quick image of something, like, a flower, a bee, or a field. Then her face pops into view. Sometimes I see her visiting me in a strange dark place."

"Where do you think this place is?"

"It's not anywhere I know." There's a sudden wind gust that rattles the cottage. "Do you love her?"

He fondles the turquoise bead on the necklace she made for him. "I've never been in love before, but I wish I could be with her or that she was here with me."

"I hope one day I will know what it's like to be loved by someone."

"When you are open to love, love will find you." He parts the curtains at the window, and Victor looks out. The snow continues to drift around the little cabin. There isn't anything to see but darkness. Victor senses another kind of darkness that can't be seen, only felt.

She stands and says, "May I hug you? This is the first night I haven't hugged my father goodnight, and it feels...it's difficult."

"I could use a hug myself." They embrace. The hug is warm and comforting for them both.

"Goodnight, Victor."

"Goodnight, Emily."

All night the wind blows without a break, and the snow grows higher and higher. The storm obscures their scent from the Simerin below, five miles north, in an old Anasazi cave dwelling, eating their scores and keeping warm by a fire.

Market

All roads lead to the center, like spokes in a wheel, to the heart of the city. Monahdah and other beings congregate for their routine visit to the market. A large portion of the markets are under the clear ellipsoid bubbles. The bubbles are transparent and provide the perfect environment for the gardens. I stand with Amari and behold all the pleasantries of the food, the aromas, and the array of all the patrons. Fruit-bearing vines grow vertically up wood trellises. A bee, the biggest I've ever seen, buzzes right by my face to enter a slit in a wooden tower. A man turns a knob and gold honey pours into a hand-crafted blue, ceramic jar. He walks straight in my direction. With large eyes that are the same color as the jar and a wide smile, he presents the honey.

Amari nods. "It's a gift."

The man bows and extends his arms out with the honey. "MiLamu Nahma."

I take the jar and bow. "Lamu Nahma." I lift the lid and smell the sweet honey, dip my index finger in the gold, and taste the honey from my finger. A tear streams down my face.

Amari puts a hand on my shoulder. "What is it?"

Overcome with emotion, I have difficulty answering. "I'm worried about Victor. I don't hear him. I don't feel him. I don't know if I'll ever see him again."

"I understand," says Amari, and she gives Anah a big hug. "I know what you're going through."

"Thank you, Amari. It's been a while since I had a girlfriend to hang out with. You're very easy to be with." Amari and I hook arms and wander through the market.

A tall, lanky, powder blue being, with an extra eye between her brow, stares at me. She gracefully glides in my direction with a basket full of exotic fruit and flowers. She proudly presents her basket with her very long, skinny fingers. She bows, turns, and drifts away like a cloud.

I pick up a piece of the pink, circular fruit from the basket and smell the ripeness. "I don't think she's Monahdah."

"A long time ago, Simerin attacked her planet, Vi. Most Vibhans died, and the last remaining survivors live here."

I hate the reminder about Simerin and the far reaches of their destruction.

A much older woman in a blue, linen robe with long gray hair, looks in my direction. Her blue hood obscures her face. "At last, you are here," I hear. The old lady puts something in her sack.

"Who is that woman over there?"

Amari turns around. "I don't see anyone."

"She was right there. I couldn't make out her face, but I could feel her eyes on me."

"People are going to stare at the only female Monahdah." Amari leads me out of the market. In the distance, drums beat from the far side of the woods. She takes my hand. "Come. It's time."

Jig

In the morning, the gang and Emily eat more stew. "How much stew do you have?" Alan chews with his mouth full.

"Enough for three days. I have a special treat on our last day here."

Hania leans closer to the table. "What is it?"

"You'll see," she says feeling clever. "How about some music?"

Willy's color has returned to his face but walks with a slight limp. "That's not a good idea, Miss Emily. We don't want to be discovered by those uglies."

With that everyone stares into space and sighs deeply with boredom. Emily goes up into the loft and brings back with her a little case. She unzips the case and lifts out a violin. "The wind is too strong, and Simerin aren't near. Victor said so."

"How do you know?" Willy looks at Victor.

"I looked."

"Like what you did at the hogan," Hania says.

Chuchip sips on a glass of water. "They could be hiding. There are lots of places to hide."

Alan finds the bottle of whiskey next to a bible above the fireplace and pours some into his coffee. "Something to help pass the time." Leaning closer to Willy he whispers, "How can a blind girl play a violin?"

Emily places the bow on the strings and plays a long, slow note that fills the room with vibration. She moves the bow slowly from one string to another and plays a mysterious, melancholy tune.

"A blind girl who can make a man cry, that's how." Willy wipes away a tear that settles in the crease of his nose.

Her bow gradually moves across the strings faster, and her fingers play more notes. Victor taps his foot to the swinging rhythm. The sound is brighter and the story more hopeful. The men slap their hands on the table as the bow moves faster, and the sound crescendos. Alan tries to dance around the room with Willy. Willy hobbles around, doing his best on his bandaged foot. The dancing and the music lifts their spirits, and the weight of their journey is momentarily forgotten. Victor picks up Emily in one swoop and places her on the table as a stage. The small cabin is filled with clapping, and stomping to the jig. Outside, the howling winds blow, swallowing up their joyful sounds.

Alan grins ear to ear. His hands tingle from all the clapping. "How did you learn to do this?"

"My father taught me. It's a jig."

"But how? If you can't see..."

"You don't need to see, silly, you need to hear."

Alan looks at Emily in a different way, a very unexpected way. He notices the way her long, chestnut hair falls past her shoulders and over her breast, her pink cheeks, and her smooth, long neck.

Emily doesn't need to see to feel the weight of Alan's stare. "What are you staring at?"

Alan's cheeks redden, and he nervously pushes up his glasses. "I was just admiring your...violin." She turns away, smiling.

The room turns very dark, and the relentless storm blows

harder than the day before. A tree in the forest breaks, creating a sudden disturbance and the horses are agitated. Chuchip lights the gas lantern, "I better check on them."

"Thank you, Chip." Emily carefully sets the violin back in the case. "Snowshoes are in the trunk."

Victor opens the trunk and takes out a pair. "I'll go with you."

Wind blasts through the doorway as soon as they open it. The snow comes up to Chuchip's waist, and the wind covers their tracks, almost immediately. The fallen tree, luckily, landed in another, preventing it from crashing down on the stable roof.

The stable door blows open and bangs against the side wall, further agitating the horses. Victor comforts them in Monahdah, and they calm down. Chuchip reaches for the alfalfa and then looks surprised. "Where did that horse come from?" He nods his head to an appaloosa. They hear rustling sounds in the straw from behind the stall door. Victor slides the door open and holds the lantern into the dark corner. Crouching in the hay behind the appaloosa is a girl with long black hair and big brown eyes, shivering under her blanket.

"Chip, help me get her into the house!" Victor moves slowly because he doesn't want the girl to feel more afraid. "It's okay. What's your name?"

The girl retreats further into the corner of the stall and hugs her legs into her body. Victor places his hand on her arm and softly says, "I'm going to pick you up and take you into our cabin where it is safe and warm. Our friend Emily has food." He slowly puts his arms around her and scoops her up. Chuchip secures the blanket around her and follows them back to the cabin. When he opens the door, Alan, Hania, and Willy look dumbfounded. "She was in the stable," Chuchip explains.

Emily approaches the doorway. "What has happened?"

"We don't know," says Chuchip. "She won't say anything."

"She's in shock," says Victor as he sets her on the cot next to the wood stove.

"How long was she out there?" Alan says. Hania, Willy, and Emily move closer to the girl.

"Long enough," Victor answers. "The snow-covered up their tracks. Just give her some space."

"Their tracks?" Alan says.

"There's another horse in the stable. I presume that's how she got here. Emily, perhaps a bowl of your stew?"

"Of course! This wasn't part of my vision." Emily feels around for the ladle. "I made plenty of stew, though, so don't worry." Emily brings a bowl, but the girl won't take it. She lays down and closes her eyes. Victor pulls up the blanket over her shoulders and places his hand on her head. He experiences the tragedy that befell the girl in her village as if it happened to him. She hides under a bed where her mother covers her with many blankets and pillows. The blue light flashes many times. She remains unharmed under the bed. When she finally crawls out, she finds her mother dead on the floor with two black holes for eyes, burned from the blue light. She searches for her father in the horse corral and finds him in the same condition as her mother. All the horses are dead, except she doesn't see her father's favorite appaloosa. The other villagers who tried to escape the light and the metal, screeching sound in the sky, all lie dead in the snow with black, hollow eyes. She runs back to her room and returns under the bed until she becomes so thirsty that she crawls out. The appaloosa returns home and stares through the window.

Her father's spirit speaks to her. "Take the horse up the trail where the wild mushrooms grow." In the storm she's unable to find her way. The snow is so thick, she's unable to see the horse's head. The appaloosa finds the stable where her near-frozen body falls off the horse.

Victor inhales deeply, troubled by what he saw. "You did well. You're safe now."

Soon after dinner, they retreat to the beds. The girl sleeps in the cot, so Chuchip doesn't mind making a bed roll on the floor. Victor and Willy lay next to each other in the dark. Willy quietly snores, and Victor is wide awake. What happened to the girl stirs the pain that he carries, and he's experiencing a feeling that he's not familiar with. A lack of confidence. He understands now that this mission has only just begun for him and is far from over. He's responsible for all of them and getting them to safety. He hopes they are all strong enough and clever enough to get there, or maybe just plain lucky enough. According to Emily's vision, they have only one more day at the cabin. It's not a matter of if they encounter Simerin but when. There's much planning to do.

Victor quietly gets out of bed, dresses in his warmest layers, straps on snowshoes, and slips out into the night.

Booby Traps

Victor opens a creaky shed door. Emily's father didn't allow anything to go to waste. It appears he was a very organized hoarder. He has stashes of everything, including rope, wire, and nails. An array of tools hang on the walls. Victor grabs rope, wire, wire cutters, the hatchet, and a saw.

"What are you doing?"

Victor spins around. Willy steps into the shed.

"You shouldn't be out here," Victor says, placing wire into his bag.

"Why are you sneaking around?"

"I tried not to disturb you. Plus, you almost lost your foot from frostbite."

"I'm fine now. What are you up to?"

"I'm making traps."

"You want to trap uglies?"

"We're outnumbered. If we are to get there in one piece, we need a strategy to outsmart them and a way to get to the lake without drawing attention. It will be difficult. Simerin are excellent trackers. If I set up traps it could buy us more time."

"I don't mind fighting."

"Our priority is to get everyone to safety as quickly as possible."

"In Nam, we set up human snare traps with grenades."

"We can't use grenades unless we want the entire Simerin army on us. Here's a hatchet. Find us some healthy branches, and we'll improvise."

The clouds part, and the full moon allows the men to work through the night. The wind has settled, and in the silence, the sound of the snow falls in the trees like tiny crystals. Willy rides the mule from location to location, and Victor walks beside them. They carve dozens of pine branches into spears and diligently set up snares throughout the forest. At the log bridge crossing, Willy sets a trap using wire and a carefully placed rock under the log. The wire leads to a snare that pulls the stick away, releasing the rock. If successful, the log bridge will fall into the rocky ravine as well as any unfortunate Simerin tracker walking across.

Before the crack of dawn, the men finish and head back to the cabin. Willy stops. Victor looks in the direction of Willy's gaze. A herd of elk, half buried in the snow, lie frozen and dead. All their eyes are hollow and black. A dozen ravens peck at their corpses. Willy gives Victor a tacit expression. Silently, they return to the cabin.

On the front porch, they remove their snowshoes and feel proud. Victor pats Willy on the back. "We accomplished much more than I could have managed alone."

"We will always accomplish more together."

"You're right. Thank you, Willy."

A Map for Emily

The village girl is awake, and Emily gives her some stew. "Did you finish your work?" she asks when they walk into the cabin.

"For now." Victor pulls out a chair and sits at the table. "The end of the storm is near."

Emily gives him and Willy a bowl of stew. "You should eat. You've been out there all night."

Victor glances at the girl, sipping broth. "She hasn't said anything yet," Emily says quietly. "At least she's eating."

Victor spoons up some soup. "Emily, do you have any maps of the area?"

She opens a drawer in the small wood desk and pulls out a trail map of the Jemez mountains detailing the rivers and valleys, elevations, and trails. Victor opens the map and spreads it out on the table. "Everyone, please join me. We need to get familiar with the area. This time tomorrow we will embark." Victor points at a spot on the map where a star is already marked. The gang gathers around the map. "This is where we are." He places his finger on the map. "This is where we crossed the log bridge and climbed the ravine with the rope." He slides his index finger along the map. "And here is where we left the vehicles."

Alan points at the map. "What's this?"

"That's a creek."

Alan feels embarrassed.

"That's okay. It's not your fault you don't know how to read a map," says Willy. "Cell phones fault."

"Just look. There's nothing to know. Here are the peaks and here are the valleys. This is our destination."

Victor wishes he could go through Los Alamos to get the Mon tablet that's locked away in a lab there. However, such a side trip is too risky. Instead, he listens to his father's voice to stick to the plan and get everyone to the underground chambers.

"How long will it take us to get there?" Chuchip asks.

"If we take this trail through the mountains, twenty hours, maybe more, depending on the weather and how well the horses do."

"When are you going to tell us what happens when we get there at this reservoir?" Alan says.

"There's food, shelter, and protection."

"The foo fighters won't find us?" Hania says.

Victor places a reassuring hand on Hania's shoulder. "We'll be safe."

"Listen closely. Willy and I made snares...booby traps." Victor points, "Here, here, and here." He marks the areas with an x. "Simerin are very good trackers, but we can easily outsmart them." Victor points at the second snare. "We will separate here, circle around this way, and meet up at the top of this ridge. That will divide any Simerin trackers and lead them into these two snares. After that, we can set more traps. The idea is to keep things undetected and covert. Do not fire your weapon unless you have no other option."

Alan crosses his arms and frowns. "How do we avoid setting off one of these booby traps ourselves?"

"The one at the log bridge, just so you know, is already set. Willy marked an x on the trees with a hatchet. That way you know what areas have traps. Don't worry. Willy will be in charge of this route."

Alan tries to grapple with reality, but this reality is still too unbelievable—the planet is under siege from very bad aliens, and they want to trap them in basic, rudimentary ways. Alan scoffs and rolls his eyes. "Don't worry! The probability of something going wrong is pretty great. We saw these aliens. I don't think sticks and stones are going to stop them. I don't like the idea of us separating either."

Chuchip shakes his head. "We are more likely to fool them if they are separated into smaller groups. We can't trap them all at once."

"That's correct," says Victor. "I've noticed they travel in groups of four. The strategy is to buy us time and gain as much room as possible to get us to the lake without being followed."

Victor senses Alan's struggle. "This is why I'm reviewing the plan with you, so you can prepare. We are in survival mode. We must be alert at all times. Your life depends on us, just as we depend on you."

"I'm afraid," says Hania. "Maybe we should just stay here."

"It's okay to be afraid," says Victor.

"But you're not."

"I am afraid. We could stay, but who knows for how long. Most likely, we wouldn't last another day here after the storm."

He looks into all their eyes. "When you're prepared, you'll have less fear. Being afraid is just a feeling, and it can't hurt you. When I'm afraid I take deep breaths, and I look to the big, blue sky." He looks into Hania's eyes. "Remember, you can go to your safe place, like you did that night of the blue flash."

They continue discussing their plans concerning food, water, and horses. Willy reminds everyone about the supplies and extra weapons in the van. They all agree to retrieve what they can.

Emily recalls her visions and sees the lake, but she has an unsettling feeling and wishes she could see things more clearly. She sees herself swimming in dark, murky water.

Her expression reflects her concern, and Victor speaks with her privately. "What is it? Another vision?"

She nods her head and whispers, "I see the lake, but I don't see everyone. There are seven of us but at the lake...I don't know. I see a lot of confusion. There's a lot of mourning and anger directed at you. It's not clear and hard to understand right now."

"It's okay. Try not to worry about the future. What happens, happens, and nothing will be your fault."

"I'm sorry, Victor. I wish I could help. Being blind will be a burden on you and everyone." She says softly, "I know I will have to swim at the lake."

"You are in no way a burden, Emily. You must know this and never say that again. You've done more for us than you know. You've given us food, shelter, and warm clothes. You helped save poor Willy's foot. You made us smile and dance with joy."

Emily sits up straighter. "Victor, can you show me how to shoot a gun?"

"I don't think that will be necessary."

"But it will be."

"I don't have a problem with it. I can show you," says Willy.

"Thanks, Willy."

After learning about gun safety, they become silent with anxiety. Soon they will have to leave their little sanctuary in the forest. Victor, however, sits on the floor and hammers the head of a nail into paper, carefully hammering it at specific areas, while intensely studying the trail map. Nobody asks what he's creating, until finally, as the creation becomes more and more intricate with embossed dots and lines from the marks he makes with the nail, Hania kneels closely. "What are you making?"

"It's for Emily." Victor turns over his creation and places it on the table.

Emily runs her fingers over the embossed dots and smiles. "This is beautiful, Victor! I can be a part of this, too. This is the nicest thing anyone has ever done for me!"

Victor guides her hand as he explains, "This means you are facing north, so if it's the other way, you're going south. The top of the map is indented so that you know which way to hold it." He continues to move her hand along the paper. "Here is the lake and this is the trail." Emily smiles as she becomes familiar with the map and the route they will travel on. "My father put that rope on the tree and taught me how to get there and back. But that's the farthest I've ever gone on my own."

"Also, there's something you should know about me," Victor announces. "I can hear your thoughts. I do respect your privacy, so I don't go around listening. Unless you're Alan. His thoughts are loud and hard to turn down. My point is, if you find yourself in duress, direct your thoughts to me, and like answering a phone call, I will hear you."

"I wish you didn't tell me that. Now I'm going to have impure thoughts," says Willy jokingly. "What am I thinking about right now?"

"You want to eat a Kit-Kat bar."

Emily closes the oven, puts the finishing touches on a vanilla pancake with frosting, and sticks a candle in the middle.

"This is my surprise," she says holding the cake. "Today is my birthday. I don't know the actual day, but this is the day my parents and I have always celebrated."

Everyone sings Happy Birthday and gathers around the table. The cake is a welcome treat after eating stew every day. The gang feels happy, and they wear smiles on their faces, even the girl from the village.

Victor takes a bite of cake. "Emily, why don't you know your birthday?"

"I was brought to the cabin. The man we buried wasn't my biological father."

"Oh, so that explains why you're..." Alan pauses.

"White?

Alan frowns. "You were abandoned?"

"I was saved."

Emily can't see their happy faces but can hear the joy in their voices. "I know it's only been three days, but you all mean so much to me. You're my family now. I couldn't ask for a better birthday gift. Thank you."

They look into Emily's cloudy eyes. Victor breaks the silent moment. "Thank you, Emily. We are family now, and you're a part of this mission."

Alan rests his fork on the plate. "What exactly is the mission?"

"To get us to safety."

"I know that, but then what?"

"Then we'll see what happens."

"Because you don't know. Right?"

"Maybe others are out there and need help," says Victor. "What I do know is that we are alive, and I can get us to a safe place."

A Beautiful Life

The moon shines on the little cabin, and the snow sparkles, contrasting with dark shadows in the forest.

"Don't be afraid," Emily whispers to the girl. The girl turns on her side to face Emily, and the girl reaches for her hand. "We will be okay."

Chuchip and Hania toss and turn and pull on the covers. They have a silent fight over their share of the blanket until Chuchip moves to the floor.

Alan stares up at the beams on the ceiling like he has for the past three nights. He focuses on something unbeknownst to him before, and he finds it odd he didn't notice it until this moment. The letters A.R.W. are carved into the beam, with the number 91 next to them. Perhaps it's the year the little cabin was built. He continues to stare at the initials. The thought of leaving the security of the cabin frightens him and stirs in him an unusual desire to read his Tanakh. He hasn't read scrolls since he was a young boy, too young to remember. Frustratingly, he tries to hear his father recite the writings. He wishes he could speak to his dad so he could remember the sound of his voice. He glances up at the mantle where the whiskey is and recalls seeing the Bible and retrieves it. Lying on the sofa, he turns the pages. The book opens to Psalms. He looks down at the page and, coincidentally, Chapter 91 is highlighted.

91 He that dwelleth in the secret place of the most High shall abide under the shadow of the Almighty.

2 I will say of the Lord, He is my refuge and my fortress: my God; in him will I trust.

3 Surely he shall deliver thee from the snare of the fowler, and from the noisome pestilence.

4 He shall cover thee with his feathers, and under his wings shalt thou trust: his truth shall be thy shield and buckler.

5 Thou shalt not be afraid for the terror by night; nor for the arrow that flieth by day;

6 Nor for the pestilence that walketh in darkness; nor for the destruction that wasteth at noonday.

7 A thousand shall fall at thy side, and ten thousand at thy right hand; but it shall not come nigh thee.

He closes the book and wants to feel the strength of the words. Without fear and with a sound mind, he sleeps.

Victor looks outside through the window, going over the details of each trap in his mind, hoping that everything goes as planned. He ponders the underground chambers. They were built just for this scenario; however, he's never actually been to them. They could potentially live there for many moons. He hasn't explained to the gang about these chambers because he doesn't want to burden them. He wants them to focus on getting there. The biggest challenge thus far. How would he convince them that they will have to hold their breath underwater for several minutes? He doesn't even know if they can swim.

Movement from behind a ponderosa crosses his line of vision. Out of the shadow steps a full-grown bull elk with huge antlers, the largest he's ever seen. Victor wants to share the moment and nudges Willy on the bed to get his attention. The two of them spy the elk in reverent silence, and the bull, almost knowingly, turns his head and stares at the cottage.

Victor turns to Willy and says, "Can you swim?"

"Uh... I can tread water."

"Underwater?"

"I don't know. It's been a long time since I've tried. Living in the desert might have something to do with it. What is this about?"

Victor looks back out the window and the elk retreats into

the shadows of pines. "We have to swim underwater and hold our breath for a couple of minutes."

Willy gets up and paces about the room. "What about Chip and Hania? What about Emily?"

"I'm mostly worried about you, Willy."

Willy sits on the edge of the bed. "This might be the end of the road for me. I don't want to go into hiding anyway. I want to fight those uglies."

"We're not hiding, we're surviving." The room becomes quiet with worry. "Hold your breath," instructs Victor.

Willy looks at Victor in disbelief and shakes his head. "I'm serious," says Victor. "Imagine you're underwater. Let us practice how long you can hold your breath."

"It doesn't matter because I already know. I can't hold it for a whole minute. Definitely not two."

"It's okay, Willy. I have an idea. I'll have enough oxygen for both of us. You just have to stay relaxed. The more relaxed you are the less oxygen the body needs. If you can hold your breath for at least 40 seconds then I can provide the rest until we get to the chambers."

Willy sighs. In his mother tongue, he says, "I don't know. I'm not a young man anymore. I've been through a lot in my life. I've seen my share of darkness, of war...strive. Fighting for the man in power for him to stay in power. The white man, the Spaniards, once invaded this land. They rounded us up, took our children, burned our crops, tortured, raped, starved us into submission like dogs. These uglies aren't any different. We've seen it all before. I don't call them uglies because of the way they look, but because they bring death, destruction, and fear. If I'm going down, I want it to be on my terms."

Victor replies in Navajo, "Willy, I think my plan will work."

Willy looks out into the illuminated night. Feeling the glow on his face, everything becomes clear. "The last trap will be mine. This will give you time to help the kids swim to the chambers. This is the only way. Don't tell the others. They don't need to know." Victor wants to argue, but Willy's mind is firm. He sits on the edge of the bed. "When one is in control of destiny, it provides peace and clarity. A true warrior is willing to make the ultimate sacrifice, a testament to survivors to live a good and honest life; a beautiful life, not an ugly one. That's the destiny I have chosen."

MiLamuKa

Five miles north, Simerin congregate around a fire in an ancient Indian cliff dwelling. The pigment, changing cells in their skin has turned into a chalky white to blend in with the snow. Their ominous shadows creep along the cave walls as they devour human flesh, feasting on their recent attack. One Sim wanders away from the group and relieves himself. He urinates over the edge of the cliff, catches a scent, and sniffs twice. He looks to the south with flared nostrils, smiling, showing all his razor-sharp teeth, and announces his discovery to the others. "Adamah neek viee."

"You scout it out and let us know," they gruff, drunk on human flesh and unwilling to depart the warm fire.

"Mi-La-mu-Ka!" The Sim cuts a trail into the forest, straight for the cabin.

The Message

Preparing for battle, Victor conditions his mind and body, moving effortlessly in and out of postures. A short distance from the cabin, a white owl sits on a branch in a small aspen grove. His round, heart-shaped face turns to look at Victor then flies away. Victor leans into the window to see where it went when the owl flies right onto the windowsill. He stares into the bird's big, round eyes, and the owl stares directly into Victor's. A cloud overshadows the moonlight, and it flies away into the shadow. Willy suddenly stirs awake and cries out. "Yá'át'ééh. Há'át'íí biniiyé?"

"It's just me, Victor."

"I was dreaming. An owl was flying in my face everywhere I went."

"There was one just outside the window. He wants to give you a message."

"If you saw it, then the message was for you as well."

"What's the message?"

"Only you can answer that," Willy whispers in the darkness. "For me, the message is clear. But it's only for me."

As Victor closes his eyes and feels heavy with sleep, the message comes to him. He will visit the spirit world a second time but won't be received until it's truly time for him to enter.

An hour before sunrise, Victor and the gang work hard at

their chosen jobs. Quietly, without any discussion, they move with purpose, packing the mule with two days' worth of supplies and more traps to set along the way. Victor steps into the snowshoes, and the others mount the horses. Alan and Emily ride her dark chestnut, River. Chuchip and the village girl are on her Appaloosa. Willy and Hania ride the buckskin mare, Bonny. Lucky, the mule, is burdened with carrying most of the supplies. They mount their steeds and head out in pairs. The snow, in some of the deeper drifts, comes up to the horses' belly.

When they reach the ridge, they turn left and follow the edge of the ravine to a place where the horses can safely descend and cross the creek.

Upwind, to the north, Victor sees a plume of smoke. He can smell the horrid wretch of burning flesh, and worse, the distinct smell of Simerin. He doesn't need to see them to know that it's a group of nearly fifty. He stops. The horses halt.

"This is the way," Alan says. "I memorized the map."

Emily's face shows a knowing fear. "Victor!"

"I know! I'll head them off. Keep going and meet me before the second trap!"

Alan nervously tightens his grip on the reins. "What? What is it?"

"Simerin are out and detected us. Just meet me near the second trap!"

Alan bumps River, and the horses push through the snow. Willy looks back and says, "Good luck," but Victor's already out of sight.

Take the Bait

Victor hides behind a large ponderosa. A Sim creeps around to the front of the cabin, and Victor takes aim with his crossbow, but the Sim steps out of sight around the back of the cabin. He sniffs around the stable and follows the horses' tracks. Victor waits for the Sim to get within range before he pulls the trigger. Two more Simerin arrive at the cabin as Victor releases his bow and hits his target in the shoulder. The Sim yells out, capturing the attention of the other two. He pulls out the bow like a splinter. Victor quickly shoots him in the heart and kills him. The others are now in pursuit, chasing him through the woods. Victor leads them to the ridge where the rope is tied to the tree and the log bridge. He slides down the rope in one swoop, landing on the ledge that meets the log crossing. He looks up. Simerin introduce themselves with a malevolent grin with razor-sharp teeth. They slide down over the snowy rocks and tree roots. Victor carefully steps over the wire on the log and then hides behind a tree where the trigger to the snare is set. They walk out onto the log and trip the wire, triggering the snare. The rock collapses, and the log jostles out from underneath them. A Sim cartwheels down onto the rocks below. The other holds on to the edge of the log. He digs his claws into the snow and tree bark. Victor runs to the log, and with all his strength, pushes the log over the ledge to finish the job. The Sim spins down into the rocks.

The gang anxiously waits for what seems like an eternity,

for Victor to return. "What's taking so long?" Chuchip says. "Should we go look for him?"

"No. I think we should wait," says Emily. "He will be back."

Willy turns his horse to face the group. "Because your visions say so?"

"My visions show him at the lake, so he must come back," she explains.

"But that might be because we have to go get him, like, right now," Alan raises his voice. "I mean, we can't just make our decisions based on these so-called, 'visions.'"

"You should argue more quietly," says Victor, snowshoeing through the snow. "I can hear you from a mile away."

"What happened?" Willy asks.

"Just as planned—at the log trap—two of them went down, and one at the cabin, but it's only a matter of time before the others notice if they haven't already. This is the place where we separate. Willy and Chip, you take this route," he says, pointing. "We'll meet on the other side. If you need me, remember, just call." Victor puts his finger on his head.

Willy, Hania, Chuchip, and the village girl, take their planned route, while Victor, Alan, and Emily head out in the opposite direction. Victor sets two more traps, and Alan follows his instructions to assist. On the other trail, Willy retraces his steps from the night before and recognizes the landmarks along the way.

Five Simerin scouts tramp up the creek and discover the Simerin bodies, mangled in the rocks of the ravine. They examine the scene, retracing the possible cause of their comrade's death. The leader recovers a weapon, glowing red. They climb up the side of the ravine and follow Victor's tracks.

Revealing his sharp teeth and black tongue, his mouth opens. "Su-dah-K!" he barks, so they follow him to the place where the gang separated. Three of them go to the left. The other two go right.

Willy finds the tree he marked with an x. The spears are well hidden in the boughs of the pine and the fresh snow.

Willy instructs Hania to dismount. "Walk the horses and Lucky over there. I'm going to set this trap." He rolls wire out across the trail and secures it carefully to a stake. When tripped, a row of spears releases, hopefully, into Simerin. If one escapes this trap, they will fall directly into the next trap.

He holds his breath for a moment and carefully backs away. "Okay. Let's go. We shouldn't..." A tree explodes right next to them, and the horses rear. Hania loses his reigns, and Bonny gallops away. Simerin fire their weapons at them from 50 yards away. Chuchip raises his rifle, but Willy puts his arm out to stop him. "Take the girl! I got this!"

Chuchip and the girl gallop away. Willy and Hania hide behind a ponderosa with a wide girth. Another shot is fired. Bark and flames explode right above their heads. Willy peeks around the tree. Three are headed right for the trap. "Come on, Uglies! A couple more steps!" The snare releases with immense weight and force, piercing one Simerin through the eye and out the back of his head. The second Sim got hit right through the neck. The last Sim remains still, unwilling to step forward or back. He looks around for another trap.

"Stay here!" Willy says and darts across the trail behind another ponderosa. The Sim fires at Willy and steps through the second snare. A spear penetrates his chest and another through the neck, wedging him between the spears of the first trap with the others. Yellow Simerin blood drips down into the snow releasing fumes. The stench burns in their nostrils. They cover their faces to avoid breathing in the fumes.

"Let's get out of here!" Hania cries.

Victor, Alan, and Emily wait for Willy and the boys. He knows something has happened, but he keeps this to himself. He stays optimistic, knowing that Willy is an experienced soldier. In the distance, running between trees, Victor sees Bonny.

Alan points. "Here they come," he says before realizing it's a horse with no rider. "Shit! What should we do?" Just then, Chuchip and the girl ride into view. Alan waves his arms up in the air. Victor whistles a calm, gentle call to Bonny. She slows down and comes to Victor. He takes her reins, strokes her buckskin neck, and says something no one understands. Bonny likes what she hears. The fear in her eyes disappears, and she lowers her head to relax.

"Simerin came!" Chuchip says breathless. "Scared Bonny off."

Victor swings his leg over Bonny's back. "Where's Willy and your brother?"

"Follow the tracks. They're back at the traps!"

Victor gallops through the forest, and a half mile later,

finds them. He dismounts. "Go to the others at the meet-up spot! Take Bonny!"

"What about you?" Hania's bottom lip quivers.

"Don't worry. I'll be right behind you."

Willy lifts Hania onto Bonny and Victor gives Willy a boost up then whistles. Bonny gallops back to the others.

Victor inspects the traps. Their work was sound. He counts three Simerin in Willy's traps and two on the other trail. He hopes this is the end of any more altercations with Simerin. Victor must utilize a Jump to catch up with the gang. Every time he does, he feels a little weaker.

When they find the vehicles, they are completely buried under the snow. Willy finds the van's door and grabs more ammunition and grenades. He puts on tactical gear—a vest and a backpack loaded with magazines, grenades, and night vision goggles.

Alan grimaces. "I thought the point is to be as covert as possible. Like, not draw the attention of the whole Simerin army."

Willy doesn't respond. Alan looks to Victor for an explanation. "It's for precautionary measures," Victor says, looking over the map. "We just need to keep moving."

Willy remounts his horse, and the gang travels northeast.

Surrounded

"Stop!" Emily blurts out.

Willy pulls back on the reins. "Is everything okay?"

Victor catches up. "What's wrong?"

Emily stares ahead as if she can see. Above the cloudless, azure blue sky, the gang views the vastness of open space. A sea of white stretches for at least 17 miles before the next tree line. "Are we at the caldera?"

Willy squints his one eye from the sun reflecting off the snow. "Yes. Why do you ask?"

"We should avoid this place." Her cloudy eyes look brighter in the light, and her voice quivers with fear.

"If we move fast, we can get to the other side," says Chuchip.

"There's a mound over there," points Emily, recalling her map. "We should get to that right away. Simerin are over there," she points to the east and then to the west. "The hill is where we need to go."

"If that's true, we're surrounded. Why didn't you warn us sooner!" Alan says.

"I'm sorry if I'm new at this. Things become clearer as they unfold!"

This strikes a nerve for Victor. "None of this is Emily's fault! Your future isn't written in stone. What happens is what happens, and that's your fate. Not what Emily's visions are or are not. I don't want to hear disparaging comments from anyone again! This is bad enough." Victor looks far into the distance, and Simerin line the distant tree line in the east. "Hurry!"

The horses plow as fast as they can through feet of snow. Victor runs behind through the trail, pulling the mule along. Hundreds of Simerin scouts approach from the east, spreading out their forces to encircle them. Armed Simerin fire their weapons. The burning lasers fall just shy of the gang.

"Keep going!" Victor begs.

Simerin create a long chain around them, several miles long.

Alan's heart pounds out of his chest. "They're hundreds of them! We're totally screwed and trapped on this hill!"

"I'll try to buy some time," says Victor.

Willy encourages his horse up the hill. "You don't have any coverage out there. At least here you have the advantage of tree coverage and higher ground."

"I understand," says Victor. "Help the others up to higher ground. I have to slow them down."

"I'm going with you," says Willy.

"Me, too," says Chuchip.

Victor gives Hania the Mule. "Get yourself and the girls to the top. We'll meet you there."

Alan looks at Emily, and he realizes that he's stricken with fear, and above all, he doesn't want any harm to come to her. "Where do you want me?"

"We can position ourselves like a compass. I'll take the east side. Willy can take the south. Chip, on the north side." Victor points. "Alan, you go over there to the west. If they come within fifty yards, retreat up the hill. I'll meet you at the top."

Victor, Willy, Chuchip, and Alan position themselves on opposite sides of the hill where they have a good visual behind some pines. Victor raises his bow and aims at a Simerin about a hundred yards away. He waits for his target to get a few meters closer. To the west, Alan hears gunfire ring out across the caldera where Willy shoots down six, now seven, Simerin. Now within range, Victor shoots his bow and pierces his target in the chest. Victor hears more gunfire at Alan's position, and now Chuchip's. Victor takes out his second, third, and fourth targets, leaving a trail of Simerin in the valley, but the Simerin chain continues to close in and tighten around them. Tree bark, smoke, and flames fill the air, making it difficult to breathe and see. At fifty yards, Victor retreats further up the hill. A Sim gets through Victor's snare with minimal injury—a spear through his calf, and he laughs six feet away. Victor grabs another arrow. The overgrown Sim jumps him, and he loses it. They roll partway down the hill, and Victor gets pinned underneath him. Victor tries to reach for his arrow, but his arm is crushed under his knee.

At the hilltop, Hania takes the girl's hand, and the girl takes Emily's hand. Their breathing is heavy, but they try to remain quiet behind a tree and a group of boulders. The sound of a branch snaps. Hania spins and points his gun. "Stay here," he whispers.

Emily reaches out for him. "Don't leave us."

Hania gives Emily a gun stowed on the donkey. "Here." He moves her hand on the trigger. "Before you shoot say, 'sky,' and I'll answer, 'blue.' That way you won't accidentally shoot me."

Victor hears a distress call in his head. It comes from Emily. He fears that he has failed them and that it might all end right here under this fat Sim. With his free hand, he grabs a rock next to his head. SLAM! The Sim takes the hit on the side of his face easily but lets up just enough for Victor to push him off. Victor grabs the arrow, jumps onto the Sim's back, and plunges it into his neck several times. The Sim falls dead onto his back.

Simerin trek up the hill and pass Victor, hidden underneath the dead Sim. Two fall into Victor's traps, but two dozen Simerin manage to breach the hill and advance through the trees.

Victor retrieves his crossbow and hears a consecutive POW! POW! POW! He Jumps to get to the top of the hill where a Sim attacks Hania. To the west, Alan must retreat to the top. Victor doesn't have time to reload his bow and must engage in hand-to-hand combat. He kicks the Sim in the face, punches him in the throat, then stabs him with an arrow right through the chest.

Another Sim rushes in, straight for Emily and the girl. Victor hollers, "Emily!" Emily's arms extend out holding the gun. She yells, "Sky!" Hania jumps away in front of the village girl. "Blue!"

Emily adjusts her aim and pulls the trigger three times in the Sim's chest. He falls to the ground right in front of them.

Chuchip and Willy ascend to the top. A mixture of fire, smoke, and Simerin blood fumigates the air. The new silence is deafening after the chaos. Victor collects the horses, and the gang gathers closely. Staying on high alert, they keenly stare through the fire and debris, expecting more attacks. Victor looks to the west, but there's no sign of Alan. "Where's Alan?"

"Don't shoot!" He comes out of the trees. His left eyeglass has a web of cracks.

Chuchip weeps and hugs his brother.

"Go!" Willy breaks the silence. "All of you! You're almost there. More uglies will come!"

Chuchip's eyes are wet with tears. "No! You're coming with us!"

"We won't go without you!" Hania cries and begs.

"This is the only way you make it to the lake!"

"You don't know that!" Chuchip sniffs and wipes his tears.

"Let me go with honor while I still can."

Emily understands the vision now. The missing person at the lake is Willy, and she wishes this to not be true. "Willy, you must come with us!"

"I can't!"

"But you're family, Willy, remember?"

"You'd be there by now without all this talk. Now go."

Emily reaches out to him, and she holds him. Alan is crying and has to remove his broken glasses. Chuchip and Hania hug him. "Please, uncle. Don't do this."

Willy speaks in Hopi. "I'm not afraid. It's okay. I'm very proud of you," he says to the boys before they part.

Victor removes a sack of food and water from the mule and gives Willy the remaining Simerin traps. They make the nakwach grip in solidarity. "I'll come for you after I get them to the lake." Willy's heart is so open he can hear Victor's heart. They stare into each other's eyes and express what words can not.

Two Thousand Years Ago

The drums beckon everyone through the woods on the west side of the city. Many have already gathered. Flames rise toward the sky out of stone pillars and gradually descend in height, spiraling toward a center. A man in a high-pitched voice chants devotional songs that echo through the valley. "Nos szusahDah ma florah AmanKi. Nos szusahDah ma florah AmanKi."

Amari puts the final touches on some flowers and ties a knot with pink, orange, green, and purple ribbons. "Do you know what he's saying?"

"He sings, 'We shall unite and prosper in peace.'" Amari places the woven flowers and ribbons that she fashioned into a wreath on my head.

I remove the crown. "It's really lovely, but I don't want to be treated like some queen." I look down at Amari's daughter, Oni, and place the garland on her. She gleefully smiles and skips to Paki, showing off her floral crown.

Yemo walks through a parting crowd, holding a flaming torch. Enchanted faces gather around. "The last time the center was ignited was two thousand years ago," Yemo says passing me the torch.

I enter the spiral with the torch, and the drummers synchronize with my every step. The chanting continues and everyone's in a transcendent state. After 15 minutes of procession, I reach the center with interlocking, glass triangles, like Victor's tattoo, and light the pillar. It ignites. The fellowship cheers and their hearts burst with joy. I observe the surreal image around me. Monahdah cry tears of joy. Hundreds of them parade and dance into the spiral, chanting, and cheering, their eyes wild with excitement. When the parade of Monahdah reach the flames, they bow and honor their union with the mysterious power of grace.

Dancing and singing commence, and we celebrate the entire day and into the evening. The full moons offer an orange glow on the horizon and forest below. Campfires dot the valley for miles. I sit with Amari next to the fire eating fruit and opening gifts. Yemo and Paki entertain us by playing a game called Bahali, a Monahdah version of hacky sack. They work together to keep the little ball from hitting the ground. Not touching the ball with the hands is the only rule. Paki and Yemo show off their skills with several tricks. Without missing a beat, Paki does a handstand while catching and kicking the ball between his feet. The ball lands on the ground and the game ends with much laughter.

Yemo adds a log to the fire. Sparks and embers ascend to the moons, and I contemplate how the creation of one thing coincides with the destruction of another—an interesting anomaly—a sacrifice, and its creation. What will burn without a sacrifice, like the wood in the fire? I'm suddenly struck by this anomaly. I question my ability to grow as a Keeper. I was born with the will, but I know what lies ahead requires sacrifice. If I'm going to be a Keeper, I want to be all in. Yemo stares at me through the flames and nods approval.

The old woman in the blue linen hood from the market

stands right behind Yemo. Her white hair blows in front of her, and the blue hood casts a moon shadow over her face concealing her identity. It's odd to see an aged person on NeuMonah. I need to move around the fire to get a better look, but someone approaches me with another gift basket.

The man bows. "Nahmah, Nahanah."

"Lamu Nahma." I turn around and look, but she's gone. "How does she do that?"

"Who?" Amari asks.

"I, also, have a gift for you, Anah." I turn around, and the old woman puts in my hand a pouch. She quickly turns away, and with the help of a staff, she's gone.

Amari and Paki lean closer. "What is it?"

"I don't know."

Yemo throws the Bahali ball and catches it. "Who is she? Does anyone know her?"

"I've seen her before once or twice," says Amari. "I heard that she's a psychic and keeps to herself." Amari leans closer. "What's in the pouch?" I untie the little bundle. My heart stops, and my head swirls.

Oni bounces onto Amari's lap. "Aren't you going to show us?" I'm breathless and afraid to touch the contents.

"This is impossible."

"Anah, what is it?" Yemo says.

Hands shaking, I lift the leather cord with the turquoise pendant. "This is the necklace that I made for Victor. Who is that woman?"

Yemo scratches his head. "I've never seen her."

"This could mean that Victor's in trouble... or that he's..."

"Don't assume the worst. It could mean anything." Yemo looks closely at the necklace. "You're sure this is the same necklace?"

"I have no doubt." I pace around the campfire. "I need to find her. She has to explain this!" Yemo throws the Bahali to Paki. "I'll go with you."

Last Bowl of Stew

Willy sets as many traps as he can. The perimeter of the hillside is loaded with grenades. He gets a visual through his night goggles. They're coming.

The first grenade explodes on the far side of the hill. They're closer than he thought. He runs to his second location and waits for the next explosion. The trap releases, sending ten Simerin flying. He marches to the next location and waits but nothing happens. Simerin are wise to the traps. Willy pulls a pin and throws a grenade down the hill on top of them before quickly running to the next location. An explosion goes off at the west side of the hill which now means all the traps have gone off except for the last one—the finale. He retreats to the south side and open fires on 20 Simerin. It's time for him to reload, but he's down to his last magazine.

60 remaining Simerin split. Half of them move to the east side of the hill. The others move to the west. Willy holds on to his mag and retreats to his hiding position behind a group of boulders. Simerin gather around the carefully placed sack

of food: Emily's last bowl of stew, a piece of cake, and a Twix bar. They can't resist the smell and pick up the bag. A sim pulls the bag away which triggers the final trap. Grenades explode, blowing them to bits. A mixture of debris—Simerin parts, rocks, and trees—rain down at the top of the hill like a volcano. Willy gets blown in the blast and lays at the bottom of the boulders. He's badly injured and doesn't know if it's day or night. He doesn't even know if he's breathing or how long he's been lying there. Hours? Days? A dark figure approaches. He clutches one last grenade in his hand and pulls the pin.

Underground Chambers

Victor and the gang stop in their tracks when they hear the grenades. A plume of black smoke rises from the caldera that's now an hour behind them. Chuchip directs his horse to catch up to Victor. "We should go back! He saved you! Now you're abandoning him!"

"We must keep going or the great sacrifice that your uncle just made will be for nothing! We must honor him by getting to the lake alive. That's what he wanted." Hania wipes his face with his forearm. Victor pulls back on the reigns. "I tried to talk him out of it." Victor feels the torment of the entire group.

When they see Victor cry, it's too much for Alan and the girls. Now everyone cries. Emily pleads, "Please... we must keep going. According to the plan, we have another ten hours."

"Letting him die was never part of the plan," Chuchip says.

In their grief, they bump their horses onward and pull the donkey behind.

The snow melts into the desert ground. The gang gains a lot of ground under an autumn, starry night. The midnight hours are met with strong wind gusts. Along the way, they find a cave and vote to set up camp to rest.

Victor ties up the horses. "We'll have to make do without a fire. We're about three hours from the lake." They huddle together for warmth, but the feelings Chuchip currently has for Victor are anything but. Victor can sympathize with Chuchip. He still carries pain from the loss of his mother and holds a grudge against his father. She saved many lives but was unable to save herself.

Before the crack of dawn, the gang repacks the mule and mount their horses. After three hours, they see light reflecting off the lake. The reservoir gleams like a beacon of hope, but Victor worries about the final leg, especially with their lack of energy and fatigue. He hasn't coached them on his plan or prepared them for the arduous swim to the underground chambers. It was never the right time to bring it up. But now they're at the lake and time is no more.

"Who likes to swim?" Victor asks.

Emily clears her sore throat. "It's okay, Victor. Just tell us what we need to do. We've made it this far. No one's giving up now."

"I know how to swim." To everyone's surprise, the village girl answers. It's the first time they hear her utter a word.

"That's great!" says Victor. "Ah...What may we call you?"

"Caili."

"Caili," says Victor. "I'm going to tie a rope around your waist. Together, we will swim underwater, but I need you to hold your breath for as long as you can. I will give you enough air to breathe."

Hania wrinkles his face. "We have to swim underwater?"

"That's how we get to the underground chambers."

"This is your great plan?" Chuchip asks.

"How long do we have to hold our breath?" Alan says.

"Only a minute." This is the first lie Victor has ever told. He knows that if he tells them the real answer they will panic.

"A minute!" Alan exclaims.

"What? Is that long?"

"Yes! Maybe not for you, but for the average human—most definitely. The body will naturally want to expel carbon dioxide long before a minute."

"That's why you'll have to let out short exhales. I'll give you air through this hose. I won't let you drown."

Frustrated, Alan takes off his glasses and rubs his eyes. "That's reassuring," he says in a very sarcastic tone. "And how will you be giving us oxygen through this hose?"

"I'm going to exhale into it."

Alan laughs. "We're dead. DEAD! We should've stayed with Willy. At least we could've taken down some Simerin with him. So, let's say this works. Then what?"

"We follow a cave that will lead us to the chamber entrance. It's warm, dry, and safe. Unfortunately, we will have to leave the animals behind."

Chuchip rolls his eyes. "That shouldn't be too hard for you."

Alan frowns at Chuchip and pushes his glasses up his nose. "Your attitude isn't helping. We all know that you're angry, but your uncle saved all of our lives back there."

"Says the pot!" Emily hates to hear the arguing and can't take it anymore. "I've heard enough!"

"It's okay," Victor puts up a hand to calm Alan and Chuchip. "I get it. You're all angry, frustrated, and tired. We all need to take a deep breath."

Alan crosses his arms. "Sorry, Emily. Willy made a sacrifice so that we could get here." He rubs his lower back, sore from riding Bonnie. "I can swim, to answer your question. But not well."

Victor strips off his clothes. "Clothes will resist and slow you down." Victor senses everyone's discomfort. "We can't afford to be modest."

"Is the water cold?" Hania says.

"Yes. But you won't freeze," he says while organizing the rope and the hose. "It's most important to move smoothly and not to swim as fast as you can, because you'll run out of oxygen sooner. Just stay relaxed."

Alan picks up the hose to get a better look at what will hopefully keep him alive underwater. "I think we should, maybe, practice this, you know, before we actually do it, so we can get a feel for it."

"That's a good idea, Alan. Who wants to go first?" When no one volunteers, Caili steps forward, removes her clothes, and takes the hose away from Alan. "I'll go."

Victor wraps the rope around her waist and ties the other end around his. "After your first inhale, you'll exhale three times before your next inhale. I'll show my fingers for each exhale and a closed fist for holding your breath." He says while demonstrating. "Then you'll inhale again through the hose. Got it?"

Caili nods her head.

Hania wraps his arms in front of his chest. "Why do we exhale like that?"

"Well, unless you're used to long holds, the body will urgently want to exhale, and this will give a little relief."

Victor and Caili face each other. Victor counts. "One, two, three." Caili gathers as much air as her little body can hold. She places the end of the hose in her mouth, as does Victor with the other end, and submerges underwater. The gang nervously wait at the water's edge. Bubbles surface to the top. After more bubbles reach the surface, there's no sign of them for a long time. Finally, near the center of the lake, their heads pop up. Victor gives a thumbs up.

"What's happening?" Emily asks.

Alan looks impressed. "They came back up. They're far out there."

"I'm taking her in," yells Victor. They both go under and disappear.

"They're going for it," Alan says.

The minutes felt like hours, and after fifteen minutes, Victor returns. He rests on a nearby rock. His chest and back expand as he breathes. Every muscle is flexed, like an Olympic athlete catching his breath. "Ok… who's next?"

Alan nervously removes his glasses and rubs his eyes. "Uh… so, like, what happened? Why are you so tired? Where's Caili?"

"What do you mean why am I so tired? I just used up more than half of my oxygen to begin with. I'm not Superman, Alan. Stop thinking that."

Alan blinks several times before putting his glasses back on. "I wish he would stop reading my mind."

Hania picks up the rope and ties it around his waist. "I'll go."

"We'll practice, first, before I take you to the chambers, like with Caili. That way you won't be standing around cold and wet."

Victor and Hania wade into the lake until the water is up to Hania's chest, but shortly after, Hania resurfaces coughing up water. "I tried breathing through the hose and swallowed water," he says between coughs.

"It's okay," says Victor. "That's why we're practicing. Try to hold your breath until I signal for you to exhale."

They go under again, but after several seconds Hania's head resurfaces, and, as before, he coughs up water. He swims to the edge, unties the rope, and shivers on a nearby rock.

Chuchip gives his brother his clothes. "If he's not going, I'm not going."

Alan sighs. "Is this the only way in?"

Victor tries to think of an alternative but knows of no other way.

"I'll try," says Emily. "I've been practicing holding my breath."

"Hania," says Victor, "Don't worry. That was just practice. Okay?" Hania shivers and crosses his arms in front of his bare chest.

Victor ties the rope around Emily. The boys nervously watch in disbelief at the water's edge. "She's blind," says Alan. "I mean, how will she do this?"

"You can't see anything anyway," says Hania disparagingly. "That's why I had trouble."

Victor pulls Emily along as he swims. She's so relaxed that she easily glides next to him. After thirty seconds, he taps her arm, signaling her to exhale. They're not far from the first entrance to the chambers, so he decides to keep going. She needs to exhale but resists the urge. He taps her arm, and she exhales a little more and receives a fresh breath from Victor through the tube. They swim through the narrow passage, and he realizes the advantage of not being able to see. This was the spot where Caili panicked and lost air, but he managed to pull her along.

With only one more minute of air in his lungs, this last step is crucial. Every second must count. He taps her arm to start the process over, and bubbles exit her nose. After ten seconds, he taps. Emily exhales and swims seamlessly alongside him. He taps her one last time, she exhales, and she receives her last sip of air. Their heads rise to the surface.

Emily removes the hose and says with heavy breathing, "Where are we?"

Victor cries with relief. "You did it, Emily! You did it!" He takes her hand and guides her up the stairs. She glides her other hand along the cold, damp wall of the cave. "I trusted you. My visions already told me that it could be done." Her legs shake as her body shows signs of adrenaline tapering off. Victor holds her steady. They walk down a long, dimly lit hall that leads to another room. This room is warm and well-lit. Emily can't see, but there are stacks of blankets and soft cushions to sit on. Caili hugs Emily and wraps a warm towel around her. She softly sings something in her mother tongue to calm her.

"When I get back, we'll take the grand tour. Just need to get the boys on board." He looks at them admirably.

Emily's cloudy eyes open wide. "Victor! They're coming!" Victor disappears down the dark hall that leads back to the cave and dives into the water.

Bearded Man

Lightening flashes, and thunder echoes through the rolling hills of the countryside. The silhouette of a bearded man stands on a rock ledge. I climb the side of the hill and step up onto the ledge, but the figure goes farther up the hill. I shield my eyes from the wind and the rain. "Hello!" The figure descends to a valley and shape-shifts into a bird. The bird wants me to follow. It leads me through the valley, and I cross over creeks and swim through a river. The bird disappears in a forest with trees so large the redwood forest pales in comparison. When I look up at the treetops, I'm staring at the ceiling in my room. I was having another dream.

I sit by the big, round window and touch the turquoise necklace that's now around my neck instead of Victor's. I can smell his sweet cinnamon scent. Lightening rips across the sky and rain drips down the window. I need to find the place in my dream and run to Yemo for answers, but he's not in his room.

"I'm in the Kalari where you should be."

I step into the kalari where Yemo and ten other disciples sit quietly with their eyes closed. "I know where I can find the old woman!"

"You're late," he replies.

Unaware of protocol, I stand stiff and look for a place to sit among the others. Yemo points with his eyes at the empty space.

I take my place between two young Keepers. No one has moved a muscle or has stolen a peek since I inserted myself into the circle. I close my eyes. I think about the mysterious woman who disappeared and my odd dream. I feel a connection with the bearded man and try to uncover clues.

My hair raises on the back of my neck. It's Yemo. Telepathically, he speaks over my swirling thoughts. *"Clear all thought and become one with the group."*

This takes me back to the first day I started training with Victor on the mesa, sitting in the sandy bottom of the arroyo, with his warm hands on my thighs and mine on his. The memory pleases me. I can feel the New Mexico sun on my face and smell the piñon and juniper trees.

Outside the Kalari, a curtain of rain falls over the entrance. Thunder cracks directly above us. I jump, but everyone else is still like a stone.

"How long are we going to sit here? I have something pressing to do."

Yemo takes a deep breath. *"As long as it will take you."*

I inhale deeply and exhale slowly, to cooperate fully this time. My heart rate settles, and my thoughts slow down. I hear something, and I deepen my concentration. The faint sound becomes clear. There's a steady SOH underneath a rhythm of HUM HUM HUM. The Keepers are chanting, Soooh Hum, and I join them.

The sound of a crystal bell penetrates my consciousness. Integration begins. The perception of individual is gone, and we become One. Several minutes have passed. How long, one can't tell. Integration doesn't know time—that illusion exists only in the dimension of existence.

When I first walked into the Kalari, I didn't have these perceptions. Now I understand. We are different versions of each other, reflections of ourselves.

Everyone bows, and we say in unison, "Nos szusahDah ma flora AmanKi."

Yemo bends down and picks up a silver object in the sand. "What's that?"

"It's for our newest Keeper, but she was late, so now she must find out another time."

"I'm sorry, Yemo, for being late." The reason escapes me for a moment. "But come on. Really. Don't be a killjoy. What is it?

Yemo attaches the object to my arm and the alloy wraps around. "An armband. Does it deflect bullets like Wonder Woman?" I laugh, but Yemo stares quizzically. He has no idea who Wonder Woman is.

"If something happens again. We'll know exactly where you are."

I cross my arms in protest. "Are you serious?"

"I'm not joking, if that's what you mean. It also provides a body shield, if activated."

"A shield against what? I thought I was perfectly safe here on NeuMonah."

Yemo leans against the post and looks to the parting clouds revealing the second sun for a few moments. "It tracks your heart rate, your mood, your—"

I remove the band. "I didn't see anyone else wearing one of these. I want to be treated like everyone else."

"But you're not like everyone else. And whether you like it or not, you will be treated differently." Yemo sighs, "This is not at all the way I thought you were going to react. Two times, now, your life was in danger."

"But you brought me here so that I would be safe. Am I not safe here? If not, I might as well have stayed at home."

Yemo looks hurt. For once he doesn't know what to say. "This is your home."

"I know, Yemo. I'm sorry, but Earth is my home, too. I have to find out what happened to Victor, if he's alive or if he's waiting for someone to..." I catch my breath. "I know you can feel it, too. He was left behind, Yemo."

Yemo briskly walks towards the northern slopes. "Let's go."

"Where are we going?"

"To the place in your dream. This woman, whoever she is, will tell us what we need to know."

"Yemo, wait! I want to go alone." I caress the turquoise stone pendant. "I need some time alone. If you could point the way."

"Take this path to the ridge and follow the trail down to the stream. Follow the stream until it joins another stream with the blue rocks. Cross over a bridge, and you'll see Mahan Jalla to the west."

"The giant forest?"

"That's where you'll find her."

Hungry Monsters

Through the murky water, Victor sees Alan sitting alone on a nearby rock. Alan looks stressed and angry.

"I tried to stop them!" He throws a rock. "They took the horses and left!"

"Which way?"

Alan points south.

"Stay here! Don't move!" Victor runs in the direction the boys took off in. A hawk circles above, and he wishes, if only this once, he could fly. His feet touch the ground with great speed. Then he feels light like he has no feet at all. He sees the terrain from above and has to remember the urgent matter. The sun shines on his back and the wind against his face. Only a part of him is consciously aware that he's shape-shifting, and his arms have become wings. He sees the boys and on the other side of a ridge march an army of fifty Simerin.

Hania shields his eyes from the sun when he hears loud screeching in the sky. "Is that bird following us? He keeps screaming... like he's lost his mind."

"Don't ask me," says Chuchip.

"Something doesn't feel right, Chip. I want to go back."

"I didn't have to come with you in the first place. I could have gone to this place where our people are and be some-where—anywhere but here. But no! I stayed with you so you wouldn't be alone!"

"I don't want to fight. I just want to go back!"

"There's nothing to go back to!" The bird is so loud now that Chuchip looks up at him.

Coiled up on a sunbaked rock, a rattlesnake warns the unsuspecting visitors with its very distinct sound of his tail. Bonnie rears, and Chuchip pummels to the ground nearly right on top of the agitated snake. Before he realizes what has transpired, he feels a burning pain in his right forearm. Bonnie runs away, and to their dismay, straight to Victor. Chuchip grabs the snake by the head before it strikes again and tosses it into Chamisa shrubs.

Mounted on Bonnie, Victor reaches for Chuchip's hand. "We must get out of here!"

"We're not going back with you. Your plan sucks!"

"Just listen to me!" Victor points. "Right on the other side of that ridge, are a bunch of hungry Simerin, looking for their next meal. These Simerin are unlike the others. They won't cook you first, nor will they kill you."

Hania's face turns white with fear. "Let's go, Chip! I can do it! Let's get out of here!"

Clutching his arm, Chuchip reaches for Victor and jumps onto Bonnie. Victor looks to the south. Simerin have reached the top of the ridge. Moving with improved speed, they head straight for them. Victor encourages the horses to stay the course.

Drool flies out of the Simerin's mouths, like mad dogs. If Victor doesn't jump within the next few seconds, they will be overrun and devoured by these beasts. His other concern— they're leading these monsters straight to the lake where Alan waits. Victor yells to Hania who's galloping next to Victor on the Appaloosa. "Hold on to me!" Victor reaches across with his hand. "Whatever you do, don't let go!" Hania grabs Victor's arm.

"Chip, you too! Hold tight!"

"Why?"

"Just do it!"

Chuchip looks back at a sight he never thought possible and wonders if he's having a horrible dream. Ferocious, hungry monsters with razor-sharp teeth, designed to tear human flesh and chomp through bones, are right on their tail. The leader rips the flesh away from Bonnie's rear with his claws and then they disappear.

Last Donkey Alive

Situated on an outcrop of rocks that looks out over the desert, Alan paces back and forth with his rifle secure across his chest. He inhales deeply and counts; one, two three, four. How long? 30 seconds? 20? He paces back and forth with every thought. "Where the hell is he? Victor wouldn't abandon us, right? Emily and Caili are in the chambers. How am I going to find them on my own?" He looks around at the vastness of open land. "I could be the only man alive." He looks at Lucky, who's really a mule, standing nearby without a care. "You could be the last donkey." Lucky puts his ears back and turns his back. Frustrated, Alan yells, "Think about that! The last donkey alive!" Alan adjusts his broken glasses on his face to gain composure. Something strange pops into view. Out of thin air, Chuchip, Hania, and Victor return, frantically galloping across the desert. Alan jumps off the rock and runs down to them. They dismount in a frenzy. Chuchip falls to the ground, holding his arm. Alan helps him to his feet and sees his arm, swollen and discolored. "What the hell did you do to him?"

Victor slaps the horses' rumps to incite them to run away to throw Simerin off their scent. "We need to go together, all at once, to the chambers. Where's the breathing apparatus?"

Alan holds out the tube. "You mean this?"

Victor takes the tube. "Put your clothes and shoes in this bag. I don't have time to explain." He turns to Hania, bends down on his knee, and looks at him in the eyes. "You can trust me, Hania. I won't let anything happen to you. Say you trust me. Say it!"

"I trust you," Hania repeats.

Motivated by terror, Chuchip and Hania are already in the lake. Drowning is now a better option than getting eaten alive.

Alan crosses his arms. "Don't we get to practice this first? What's going on?"

Victor cut the tube into three equal parts and tapes his ends together into one section. "Listen to me. Practice time is over. Simerin, whatever these creatures are, are on their way. I'm going to use every bit of oxygen I have. You will probably need to resuscitate me."

Before Alan can protest, Victor, Hania, and Chuchip take a deep breath and go under. The tube is much shorter, so they must swim close together. Victor puts up his finger to signal the first exhale. They swim for another ten seconds, and Victor puts up two fingers, but Hania needs air, so Victor signals for them to all breathe through the tube sooner than he antici-pated. They reach the small opening that leads them through the tunnel and into the cave. They separate to swim through the narrow passage. Victor uses the rope to guide them to the other side. In single file, they follow Victor and the rope through the dark.

Victor's vision becomes impaired. He struggles to swim. Pinholes of light is all he can see, and the holes of light are getting smaller and smaller. He tries to focus and remain calm, but his body begs for air to the extent that he feels excruciating pain. Slipping away into black ink, he hears two loud knocks and thinks he's back home on NeuMonah. He walks through the forest path that leads to the meadow where Monahdah come together for festivities. He sees a beautiful woman with long brown hair and hazel eyes. He knows these eyes! He wants to go to her, but when he tries, she only gets farther and farther away. He tries to run, but it only creates more distance. If he doesn't reach her, he will die.

Alan struggles. Completely out of oxygen, he looks up and sees the surface. He can't think of anything except breathing. When he reaches the top, he gulps and tries to remember what he is supposed to do next. His inability to focus is interrupted by a chorus of gasping breaths echoing off the cavern walls. Hania reaches the steps with his brother right next to him. He points into the pool of water and screams, "Victor!"

Chuchip dives down into the water. Victor's lifeless body floats under the deep end of the pool. Chuchip wraps his arms around his waist, pushes his feet against the floor, and lifts the dead weight upward. Alan takes Victor's arm, and together they pull his body up onto the steps. Alan blows air into his mouth. Chuchip feels for a pulse but there is none. He beats his chest. Alan continues mouth-to-mouth resuscitation.

Hania, fraught with fear, covers his face. "He'll come back, right, like before? Can he die?"

"Of course he can die!" Chuchip turns Victor's body onto its side. Victor spits up a lot of water, coughs, gags, then breathes again. He attempts to prop himself up onto his forearm and says something in his Monahdah language. He looks at the boys. "Where did she go?"

Alan looks at the others for some clarification. "Where did who go?"

Alan sits on the cold, hard stone floor, breathing hard. "We're in the underground chambers." Alan looks around with a grimace. "I don't know how you expect anyone to live here. Where's Emily and Caili?"

"We're not in the underground chambers yet," he says sitting up and gaining clarity, beads of water drip down from his long, wavy bangs and over-grown facial hair. He unties the bag around his waist and retrieves their clothes. Victor pulls over his long-sleeved shirt. "Let's hope we'll never do that again. I'm beyond proud of you boys. Thank you for saving my life—again! I can't believe we did that!"

Alan dries off his glasses with his shirt and puts them on. "I mean, maybe it's because I'm half-starved and delirious, or because my glasses are broken, but there's something I can't believe, either."

Chuchip zips and buttons his jeans. "What can't you believe?"

"You guys appearing out of thin air. There was nothing then, POP! There you were. I would like to know how that can be true, or was I hallucinating?"

"It happened," says Hania pulling his shirt on. He curiously looks at Victor. "And the bird, too, right? You were that hawk, flying over us, warning us about the uglies coming."

Chuchip cries out in pain when he tries to raise his arm to put on his shirt. Victor takes Chuchip's arm into his hands. The discolored veins have traveled farther up his arm from the snake's venom. Victor massages his arm in a downward motion. After a few minutes, the black veins fade and the swelling recedes. "That should be good until we get to the chambers."

Chuchip presses his lips together and looks down at the ground. "Sorry that we took off like that. It was reckless. I put us in danger."

Victor puts his hand on his shoulder. "You didn't know that. Despite being Monahdah, I don't know many things. I don't know why we're all here and still alive. We shouldn't be, but we are. Perhaps it is fate, unconsciously controlled by us, or by a force that no one will ever fully understand. A question with no answers. You took a risk, and you were just trying to save your brother. You and I are very much alike. In fairness, we wouldn't know about those new creatures. Now we do."

Alan frowns. "What are you talking about? What creatures?"

"They aren't like the Simerin we fought in the caldera. They're a new breed of Simerin. Created to hunt." Victor combs his thick wet hair back away from his face with his hand. "Come. Emily and Caili are waiting. They are deeply worried by our long absence."

Web of Time

I stand on the rock ledge at the top of the ridge, the same one in my dream, looking down the valley. The stream meanders through the tall grasses and abundant wildflowers. A herd of white deer graze, unafraid when I walk by. One in the middle lifts her head acknowledging my presence. Their fluffy fur moves with the breeze. I walk along the stream with the blue rocks, cross a bridge, and finally, to the west, I see the forest, Mahan Jalla. The trees are huge. As I wander deeper into the forest, they increase in size. Some have even grown together, married in clusters, taking up an enormous amount of space like houses. The soft, deep purple, feathery leaves swish on their boughs and litter the ground a foot deep.

In the distance, the old woman in the blue dress walks along a narrow pathway. She feels her hand along the smooth white bark of a tree, and I follow. Carved markings on the trees seem to guide her along the way. She turns right and left, then she's gone. I look in every direction. I hear the faint sound of singing. It comes from the other side of the tree. I press my ear against the trunk, and it seems to come from within the tree. I walk around the enormous perimeter of the trunk until the singing gets louder. There's a small opening. To enter, I must crawl. My eyes adjust to the only source of light, a small natural window from above. "Hello?"

A match ignites a lantern. The lantern reveals the old woman's face and the space inside the tree. The hollow tree is a large room where this woman has made a cozy home.

"I've been waiting for you, Anah. Come sit with me." She removes her hood, and her hazy, white eyes glow in the lantern light.

I sit on soft cushions, large enough to be a bed. "How do you know my name? Who are you? Where did you get this necklace?"

The old woman dishes out two bowls of soup and gives me one. "I know you have many questions. I'm hungry and feeling very tired today. Do you mind if we eat first?"

One slow sip at a time, she eats her soup. She puts her fingers into the soup and takes out a piece of vegetable. A small creature scurries across the floor and takes the treat. "My name is Emily," she says.

"It's nice to meet you, Emily. I'm... well, you already know my name."

Wrinkles frame her milky eyes when she smiles. "It's so nice to finally meet you."

"I don't think you should be living out here like this...with no one to look after you."

"I was waiting." The woman takes a deep breath. She reaches for my hand. "Now the waiting is over."

"By the looks of it, you've been waiting in this tree for quite a while."

Emily picks up the lantern and shines the light onto the tree where she etched marks. "This is the day I arrived here." She moves her fingers across the marks. "This is today."

"You've been here for over sixty years?"

"Then how did you get this necklace?"

"Victor told me to give it to you."

I catch my breath. "How's that possible?"

"Shhhh... let me tell you the story. And then if you have any questions, you may ask."

Emily begins her story. Victor didn't make it back to the ship with the Chantallah, as I suspected. My mother was in danger, so he lured Simerin away before they encountered my mother and her two companions. He crashed in a canyon where he was rescued. Two Hopi boys, their uncle, and Alan, found him.

"Wait! What? Alan? What's he doing there!"

"He was a bit fixated on your disappearance." I listen intently and in disbelief. Emily's visions allowed her to prepare for their arrival at her cabin, and, most likely, their survival. Through tears, I laugh at the part when they sang and danced to the violin. In harrowing detail, Emily describes the battle in the caldera against the Simerin. They lost Willy, which almost tore them apart, but his sacrifice ultimately saved them, giving them time to swim to the elaborate, underground tunnels where they've been living for nearly ten Earth years. "Victor went back for Willy but never found him, and—"

"And what?"

"That turquoise necklace was hanging on a branch."

"It must have fallen off, during his fight with the Simerin."

"It was peculiar because he was wearing the necklace. The same exact necklace. It's also strange that I didn't see it. I didn't know Willy would end his life trying to save us, and I often wonder why that is."

While Emily reaches the end of her story, I shake my head. "Forgive me, but, given your age and condition, how did you—I mean how old are you?"

"I was only 18 when this happened. I don't understand completely but something happened when we jumped. When we got here, we were back in time. I decided to stay, and Victor went back."

"I've experienced a jump like that before. It's very dangerous."

"Like when you and your brother jumped on a Simerin ship?"

"Exactly. So how were you able to jump like that?"

"Victor didn't know. He said it was very curious as if I had the capability, but that's not possible. I'm not Monahdah."

"You didn't go back with him. Why?"

"The jump took every bit of my energy. Victor called it life force. I was afraid to hinder Victor's timeline. Anyway, I was happy to stay on NeuMonah. I'm blind but living underground wasn't for me. Victor and the others saved many lives. It became an obsession for him. Victor got word of your rescue mission, but something went wrong. We waited, and you never came."

"Do you know why?"

"Simerin made it impossible to enter Earth's atmosphere. Ships are unable to arrive. Think of it like a great moat around the planet."

"Is there a way to breech it?"

"That's what Victor and the others tend to find out. I'm telling you because you need to know. The first rescue attempt fails. A few years afterward, the survivors became divided between those who wanted to leave and those who wanted to stay and fight the Satans."

"You mean Simerin?"

"Satans are new Simerin. They are much worse."

I try to imagine something worse than Simerin. "Victor was in support of those who wanted to leave with our rescue team?"

"He supported all of us. He advised us and often asked for everyone's opinion. We would vote and discuss issues."

"Like what?"

"We wanted to recover the Mon that was hidden in the labs, but he said it was too risky. He was deteriorating, and the others wanted to devise a plan to recover the Mon. Victor said it was too far and too dangerous. We voted, and we were short one vote."

"Victor's?" I ask. Emily nods. "He didn't have any Monahdah capabilities at this point?"

"Some. He chose to reserve it, in a way of speaking, for when it was imperative." Emily sighs deeply. "And it was."

"Because you had to jump."

"Yes. I was weak, and I decided that I would stay here on NeuMonah because he had to return before the way closed or else he would never get back."

"You've been here before the Simerin invasion, then. Did you warn them?"

"Victor didn't want me to say anything. It was best to not alter anything. He said it could change his path—his future or his past." Emily pours tea.

"Then why give me his necklace and make me come here?"

"It was in my vision, since I was 18, living in the cabin. Victor knows this."

"What about Alan...Is he still alive?"

A tear falls on Emily's face. "I miss him. We fell in love. My visions tell me that I see him again."

"Then, the rescue mission must succeed. Right?"

"I'm not sure." Emily's eyes look heavy and she yawns. "Maybe I'm daydreaming. In my old age, I can't tell the difference." Emily takes my hand. "I saw this encounter with you many times and now...is it real? Are you real Anah?"

"Yes. I'm real. I feel terrible that I wasn't with you all." I wipe my cheeks dry.

"Is Victor in your visions?"

Emily slowly nods her head. "My visions are different since we parted ways. He won't abandon them...all those that were left behind." Emily stares at me as if she can see clearly in her mind's eye. "Since you got to NeuMonah, I've had a vision that is very odd."

"Odd how?"

"You're covered in mud. And you appear to have a difficult time. I've learned to not think too hard on these visions now. It will make sense in time."

"I'm having a difficult time?"

"And there is someone with you. They're also covered in mud. I think I know this person. But I don't know, yet, because you're both covered in mud."

"How do you know that it's me?"

"I know it's you because I see your braid and feather."

"I don't have a braid or a feather."

"Oh, but you will."

I stare into Emily's white eyes for answers. "Maybe it's Victor?"

"I wish I knew the answer." Emily holds my hand firmly. She closes her eyes. "I'm very tired." I pull a blanket over her small frame, and she grabs my arm. "Please stay here with me tonight. I don't want to be alone."

"You should stay with us in my father's house."

"I feel safe here in the forest."

"You will be safe, Emily."

"Trauma is a funny thing, especially at a young age. This is where I live, and this is where I'll die. I feel at home here with my trees. They won't hurt me."

Emily sleeps. I stare at the etches she made on the inside of the tree and touch the day she arrived with Victor. In a flash I see him, wandering in the forest with Emily when she was young. His hair is long, and he has a beard. He looks taller and leaner, but his eyes are the same aqua blue. The image goes blank, and so does he. If only I could go to him like touching this mark on the tree. I control the sudden urge to Jump. That didn't go well before. I look at the carved circle representing my visit and all the marks and symbols in between. If I want to be with Victor again, this is the best timeline.

TuLah

"Peace comes within the souls of men when they realize their relationship, their oneness, with the universe and all its powers, when they realize that at the center of the Universe dwells, Wakan-Tanka, and that this center is really everywhere. It is within each of us." —Black Elk

I sit next to the fountain and process my encounter with Emily. Because of circumstances that I didn't feel I had control over, Victor and I are worlds apart. We've only been together for a fleeting moment in time compared to how much has happened since we've been apart. I'm running and hiding, and he's fighting and surviving. I feel angry. My father left him behind. There's no excuse. My anger builds, and I pace about the atrium.

Yemo joins me in the atrium. *"What happened to Victor could happen to any one of us. It's the risk we take as Keepers. Your time on NeuMonah will benefit you for training and for when we go back to Earth. That is if you want to be a Keeper."*

"When will we go back?"

"We wait for the Chantallah to get here. Meirlies will have a plan. We plan to be ready. Including you."

"I know you're right, Yemo, but I'm frustrated." I sit back down next to the fountain and gain composure. "Yemo, remember that night at Mom's when Victor chased after you, you know, before we met on Halloween night?"

"I managed to get away from him quite easily."

I roll my eyes. "Anyway, what I saw was a deer—Victor and a deer."

"I knew you were going to ask me about this one day."

"I want you to teach me."

"I'm not the teacher for this."

"Then who is?"

"He's a Native American shaman, a Monahdah, and six hundred years old. His name is Dihi." Yemo bends down to a red flower that's similar to a rose and inhales deeply. "This scent reminds me of Sophia," he says to himself.

"When did you learn?"

"I started as a boy. My mind was very open to TuLah."

"TuLah? Is that Magic?"

"A better translation is Source or God-power. They're not magic tricks. One doesn't learn Tulah by reading a book and then you do it. It can take years of practice. TuLah is a whole different state of awareness. One that requires extra eyes of perception."

"You think it's too late for me to learn?"

"You used TuLah before. You changed the traffic light while I chased after Sahn."

"That Drohan turned himself into a little rat, which means he knows this Source."

"You don't have to have good intentions to know it and use its power. But you will be rewarded if you use it for the greater good."

Yemo holds my arm for a moment, and I see the way to Dihi. "Thanks, Yemo."

After an hour's hike through the woods, I follow along a winding pathway and cross a stone bridge that arches over a spring. Little gray, furry creatures with large paws and long, twitching noses munch on yellow flowers. Straight ahead, a small, mud house curves into the hillside. Wind chimes of various found items, animal bones, shells, and feathers, decorate a nearby tree. Intricate stick symbols, and woven sculptures from willow branches, hang down in the windows. An eye, made from hundreds of smooth river stones, decorates the outside wall of the house. I must step through the center of the eye to enter. I feel apprehensive. My spine tingles. I hear, "How long shall I wait? Please, come in and join me."

I step through the eye, and pleasant, soft light fills the room. On a table are various dried plants, herbs, rocks, and crystals. A large hand drum sits on a chair. A strikingly tall man, with long, dark silky hair, and rich brown eyes, greets me. "It's a pleasure to finally meet you, Anah."

"It's nice to meet you, Dihi. Did Yemo tell you I was coming?"

"I sensed your visit would soon arrive. The teacher prepares, and the student comes." He leans down to examine my turquoise pendant. "This is a very special stone. Where did you find it?"

"In a village in New Mexico. I made it—"

"For Victor." He continues to stare at the stone and then directly into my eyes. "You're here to learn TuLah."

"Well, specifically, I want to know how to shape-shift."

"This isn't something one can just learn. There isn't a manual. Even if there were, that doesn't mean one would have success."

"My brother has this ability. I didn't see him shape-shift. A Monahdah with ill intentions turned into a rodent. That I did see."

"Great Spirit can't control our will, especially after one has already gained such powers. But this abuse doesn't last. The universe has a way of correcting."

"Can I choose an animal or practice shifting into a certain animal?"

"The animal chooses you," he says as he burns a plant that smells like sage. He allows the smoke to drift into the space around us.

"I don't have to do anything? One day it just happens?"

"You have to invoke all the powers of the universe in every direction." He walks around a table and gathers items; herbs, stones, seashells, feathers, and places them into a drawstring pouch. "When you connect with the spiritual dimensions of creation, Great Spirit may find favor." He closes the drawstring and ties a knot.

"I don't understand. What directions?"

With a staff, he draws a circle on the dirt floor and divides the circle into four quarters. In the center, he draws another circle. With his staff, he points to the center. "You may start here. Wait for a sign that you have permission to enter."

"Like what kind of sign?"

He gives me the pouch. "You'll know."

"Okay... still a little vague, though. What do I do with these?" I hold up the pouch.

"I don't know. This isn't my quest. It is yours."

"So, this is some kind of quest? Like a vision quest?"

"If you choose," he says leading me out of the house and into the backyard.

"How long will this take?"

"As long as you wish." He points to a large stone circle in a field. In the center stands a big, white pillar. "There's the center." A sudden forceful air blows back his long, silky hair. "The center represents Great Spirit. Great Spirit gives us emotions to guide us. One must only pay attention. Sometimes, it's okay to allow your strength to be your weakness and your fears to be your strength."

"That's quite the dichotomy."

"One day you will understand."

I precariously enter the circle and instantly feel a vibration. The closer I get to the pillar the stronger the sensation. The ground trembles. Is there something I should say or do? I look up at the pillar that towers 20 feet above me. "Hello. I'm Anah." It feels strange speaking to a rock. I retrieve a white rock out of the pouch and place it on top of a pile of white rocks from previous seekers.

My necklace lifts off my chest, and the turquoise stone pulls in one direction. I take this to be a sign. Like a magnetic force leading me, I follow, and I begin my quest.

After two days in Mahan Jalla, I find the next pillar, a lone silhouette against the rising sun. Items left by other travelers scatter the ground at the foot of the pillar. There's an inscription carved on the surface. In Monahdah, the symbols read, "Zieldah Zi." It means, your intention lies in the heart.

I lie down on the grass waiting for something to happen—a voice, a thought, a sign, or anything. The sun is directly above me. The other sun is on the eastern horizon.

I open the sack and empty the contents onto the palm of my hand. Soft, fluffy seeds pore out. I want to find a perfect spot for them. Indecisively, I walk around, unable to make up my mind on the best place. I remember what Dihi told me, "Let your strength be your weakness and your weakness your strength." I open and hold out my hand. The western wind lifts the seeds into the air, and they sail away to their new destination.

Each night, I gain more familiarity with the NeuMonah sky while sleeping under the stars and the moons. There are three other planets in this solar system, and NeuMonah has two suns and two moons. Looking up at the stars, I think about Earth, the amazing, little blue pearl in space, thousands of light years from here. It's been a long time ago since I was there, and I'm homesick. Maybe it's natural to long for something familiar when everything is new and you want comfort. I close my eyes and see my mother. Her hands turn the page of her romance novel. Her blue eyes reading the words. I fall asleep and dream.

I'm screaming. I'm cold and no longer feel the other me, my brother. I was just born. I want to go back into the darkness and the warmth. Yemo doesn't make a sound. I breathe the cold air through my nose and stop crying when Yemo is next to me. We suckle the sweet milk.

When I wake, I look up at the sky, pink clouds floating. I pack my bag and continue my trek. I'm ready to move onward to the next stone.

Southern Stone

A heavy rain has set me back at least a day. I slip and fall down a muddy ravine. I claw the saturated walls and slide back down again. Water collects at the bottom, and it's almost up to my knees. I tackle the wall on the opposite side and find a root to hold on to. The root snaps, and I splash back down. Did I come this far only to drown in this ravine? The water rises to my chest. The rain erodes the slope, exposing more tree roots. Moving from one root to the next, I use the roots like ropes to pull myself up the wall of the ravine. I clamber back to the surface and rest on my back, laughing hysterically.

My feet slosh in my boots with every step, so I take them off. It feels good to walk barefoot in the cool mud until it dries in the hot sun and cracks on my skin. I consider going back. But with clear skies ahead, I tie my laces, drape my boots over my shoulder, and trek on. Twenty miles later, the massive, southern pillar is in sight.

Leaning my back against the blue pillar, I gaze up at the sky and feel the ground underneath me. I retrieve a clear, iridescent stone from the sack and hold it in my hand for several minutes. A force comes to me from the center pillar, the one representing Great Spirit. I'm compelled to put the stone close to my eye like a lens, and I look through the stone. A person walks in my direction. When I don't look through the stone the figure isn't there, but when I look through the stone again the figure reappears. With his thick caramel hair and his aqua-marine eyes, I recognize the person as Victor. He walks and walks but, oddly, never gets any closer. This stirs much frustration and anger. I go to him, but he only gets farther and farther away. I scream because it's so infuriating. I yell at Great Spirit, "Why are you tormenting me? What is your problem?" I throw my body onto the ground and pound the ground with my fist. "What have I ever done to you?" I take the stone and throw it as hard as I can.

After a restless night at the foot of the pillar and an early morning visit from a family of night crawlers with glowing green eyes, I pack up my belongings and go west. I'm glad no one witnessed my child-like temper tantrum. I ponder Dihi's wisdom; allow emotions to guide you. I have a lot of anger stemming from my lack of trust and fear, making it hard to love properly. I realize that I've been afraid, and suspicious my whole life. If I learn to trust maybe that will bring us together. Or maybe it's a message to let go, to not care so much, because I'm tormenting myself by wanting something that isn't possible right now. With a mixed bag of emotions, it's difficult to determine what anything means.

Brilliant Dancer

"The infinite—free, unbounded, full of joy is our native state." —The Upanishads

Day seven of my quest, and the western trail has been a steady incline. The farther I go, the higher and steeper I must climb. Navigating around rocks and boulders, a sheer rock cliff confronts me. Climbing up doesn't seem likely. Going around is the best option, which will take a few hours. When I finally reach the other side of the cliffs, there's a much higher, mountainous terrain to conquer, and the last daylight begins to fade, so I make camp for the night.

Every which way I move, my body finds sharp, edgy rocks to lie on. I draw my knees into my chest and watch the half-moons rise above the clouds. Light reflects on the smooth surface of the boulders. They twinkle and shimmer in the darkness like stars. I think my tired eyes and ears are hallucinating, and I'm having another dream. Mysterious tones emanate from the rocks. Under the layers of mud, I have goosebumps. I move like a brilliant dancer, naturally choreographing around the rocks to the haunting sounds. In a half-altered state, I feel free of inhibitions.

Like a curtain, clouds drift across the moons and block the light. The magic music stops and the twinkling rocks fade. The only sound is my breath. A feeling erupts deep within my belly, and I'm mad with joy.

I pack up camp before the rise of the first sun and continue the ascent. The ground comes loose, and a cascade of rocks tumbles. I never had a desire to rock climb, and here I am, taking a crash course—literally. There's no more going around obstacles. It's either going back the way I came or finding a way up the final twenty feet of this bluff. I carefully examine cracks and footholds and tie my belongings securely onto my back. I'm not going to allow fear, one of my weaknesses, to prevent me from finishing this climb, but I don't want to be stupid and break my neck.

Halfway up, I discover a narrow space between two boulders where I wedge my body and shimmy up. But now I'm wedged between the rock walls, unable to go up or down. I try not to panic. The crack widens as it goes deeper into the rock, so, I slowly move myself inward. I pivot so that I have hands and feet on either side. Little by little, I scale between the walls for the last ten feet. Triumphantly, I climb to the surface and have a celebratory dance at the top. The big prize? The view! I'm above the treetops and as high as the clouds. I can see the kidney-shaped coastline and the giant forest to the east. Far in the distance, I see where my quest began and the huge white pillar in the center. But where's the western stone? It stands down below the first cliff near the moon rocks, not far from the spot where I danced to their mysterious music. I didn't have to climb up here! However, I'm not sorry. I'm happy here on this peak.

To consecrate my climb to the top, I retrieve the flint rock from my sack. I strike the flint until sparks catch in a pit that has housed many fires before. The clouds in the sky are ablaze with the setting suns, and, as the sky darkens, the smoke and the sparks dance upward to the crimson sky. For the first time since arriving at NeuMonah, I feel at peace. I look out as far as the eye can see to where the ocean and the horizon meet in the south. With loving arms, the mountains in the north extend to the east and west. The fire flames crackle and dance. Softly, I sing.

MiLamu Nahma AmanKi
MiLamu Nahma Nahanah
Ma Mon Ma Mon lah Monah Nahmah

Reborn

O mysterious and incomprehensible Spirit! In the depths of my heart, there is only You—You, for all time. — unknown

My heart feels as big as the sky. I smile through the cracked, dried mud on my face. It's day nine of my quest, and the black, northern stone reflects on the water of a lake. SPLAT. A huge raindrop lands on my head. I look up at a raincloud that's about to burst. I remove my clothes, plunge into the lake, and wash away layers of caked on mud. Floating on my back, I close my eyes and allow the rain to shower over me. A long, silver fish jumps, another, and another. I swim to the edge to avoid getting slapped in the face and watch this strange phenomenon. The rain cloud drifts eastward, and the warm suns' rays return. I sit on a large, steamy rock to dry and wring out my clothes.

One last item remains in the sack—a small, decorative knife. I admire the stone facets on the handle and place it next to me on the rock, not knowing what to do with it.

I bask in the effects of the past nine days with new heightened awareness. I know without knowing, feel without feeling, hear without hearing, and see without seeing. I want this feeling to last forever and never fade when I return to reality. This experience is as powerful as it is fragile. I wish to hold onto this experience when the idea of peace isn't tangible and store it deep within me, safe forever.

When I rest my eyes, I see animals that I've never seen before on land and in the sea. Some are familiar to Earth. I'm flying in a snowy forest, near a little cabin. I see my reflection in a window, and I'm a great white owl. I run with wolves and swim with animals in the sea. Creatures from NeuMonah greet me in a field and invite me to run, fly, and swim.

Light reflects off the lake, and I open my eyes. The surface of the water is like glass and mirrors big, white clouds, and a clear blue sky. I hadn't seen my image for the past nine days, and for a moment I didn't recognize myself from the water's edge.

I retrieve the little, stone-faceted knife and begin to cut. Except for a long lock, I slice away my hair. Ibraid the uncut section that drapes over my shoulder. A flock of birds flies to the coast, momentarily blocking the sun. Blue feathers fall to the ground. I use one to don my braid.

Law of One

"You are every thing, every being, every emotion, every event, every situation." The Law of One

Finally, I reach the center pillar where my journey began. The ground underneath me trembles, and my anxiety and fear has been replaced with reverence and respect. From my sack,

I remove a lock of my hair and place it under the enormous, white pillar. I place my hands on the pillar and look up at the deafening sound of the birds. Hundreds more have joined the flock. I feel light and momentarily disoriented. I'm above the trees flying next to the birds. I land in a tree in the forest and enjoy the sweet nectar of blue-speckled fruit, pecking and digging out the flesh with my beak, eating the sweet seeds in the middle.

Chantallah

Yemo is overjoyed to see me and says he resisted the temptation to rescue me from the mud cliffs. He does wish he rescued me from cutting all my hair.

"It's just hair Yemo. It will grow back. Why do you have an opinion about my hair, anyway?" I bite into a crunchy yellow root.

"I don't have one of those... opinions."

"It's...you know, just a way to shed the old me and make room for the new me. It was symbolic and felt appropriate at the time."

Paki buoyantly enters the room. "Welcome back! Nice head."

"Thanks! Yemo seems to have a problem with it."

"It makes a statement. Like, don't mess with me or I'll kick your ass."

"Thanks, Paki, but I'm not trying to make a statement, though."

"I came because I have good news! Chantallah will begin

arriving before the next moon! We're making preparations, but there is still much work to do."

"I'm going to Amari," I say on my way out the door. "I'm helping her with the preparations. Catch you later."

Yemo furrows his brow. "Why would she want to do that?"

Paki laughs. "'Catch you later' means she'll see you later."

Yemo crosses his arms and purses his lips. "There's something different about her."

"Everyone changes after a quest." Paki smiles and pats Yemo on the back. "Come. Let's go and make ourselves useful."

Hundreds of pilots dock their pods, and the first of the Chantallah begin to arrive. The Hopi families are happy and overjoyed to set their feet on solid ground. They receive food, supplies, and seeds for the upcoming planting season. They'll soon choose their new settlement. This was their main concern, finding fertile land to grow their crops. They brought their seeds and want to start their plantings as soon as possible and bless the new land with ceremony.

When I enter the new Hopi village, I'm proud to see everyone building, planning, and tilling for corn and fruit trees. I brought a welcome basket of produce for Hani and Chuchip's parents and approach a group of workers. They're in a small pit constructing adobe bricks, like back home.

"Hello." I wave my arm in the air. "I'm here to speak to the parents of Hani and Chuchip." Everyone in the pit freezes as if they couldn't believe what they heard.

A tall man and a short woman with a round face approach.

The man lifts his chin and looks down at me. He says in his language, "How do you know our sons?"

"I'm here to tell you...your sons are alive. They're okay."

The woman's hands shake, and she buries her head in her husband's chest. The husband leads us to the foundation of their house with the first footers of bricks, and we sit. "Please tell us what you know," he says.

"I met someone who spent much time with them. The boys survived, and they saved many others. Chuchip is a father. You're grandparents now. You have a grandson."

She is emotional and unable to speak. He puts an arm around his wife. "We would like to speak with this person,"

"Her name is Emily. She may be willing to speak with you, now that you're here."

The wife sniffs and wipes away her tears. "Where are they?"

"They live underground in chambers. They are much older than you remember, though, ten years or more."

The woman shakes her head. "But it hasn't been that long since we left."

"It has been on Earth."

I hand her the gift basket. "You should be very proud of them. They saved someone very dear to me. Together they were able to save many others." I hug them goodbye. "My name is Anah. Please let me know if there's anything I can do for you."

"Thank you, Anah. This means everything. Let us know if there's anything we can do for you, as well."

Scream to the Heavens

Yemo and I run to the coast. The main ship has arrived. Thousands of Chantallah will disembark onto NeuMonah. This is the ship Victor would've been on and have mixed emotions. I'm sad he's not here. But Mom is, and I want to scream it to the heavens. It truly feels like a miracle. Hundreds of pods are arriving at the southern docks. Men, women, and children, clean and well-fed, disembark from transports.

I scan the faces in the crowd and lock eyes with her. "Mom!" We weave through the crowd. I've never felt so much joy and relief at once. We embrace and burst into tears.

"I'm sorry! I'm so, so sorry that I left the way I did."

"It's okay. It doesn't matter. What matters is that you're safe, and Yemo, too." She hugs Yemo. "I'm the one who should be sorry."

"You have nothing to be sorry for, Mom," says Yemo. "I took Anah. I made her come here."

"You did what you were supposed to do. But Victor, he didn't make it back to the ship because of me."

"Mom," I take her hand. "Don't put that kind of guilt on yourself. It's not your fault. The important thing is that you're here. That's all that matters now."

Mom's face suddenly lights up as she looks at us. "I have a surprise for you." Mom turns around and says, "You can come out now."

A beautiful blond with a perfect smile steps down onto the dock. "Finally! I thought you forgot about me."

"Sophia!" We hug, laugh, and cry. Yemo and Sophia passionately kiss. He gets so choked up that he's unable to speak.

"Where's Meirlies?" I scan the crowd.

"He's very excited to see you and will be joining us." Beverly sighs and rubs her forehead. "Can we go? I feel dizzy and a little nauseated."

I look for belongings and notice they're not carrying anything. "Where are your belongings? Do you have a bag or anything?"

"It wasn't like that. It happened so quickly. We didn't have time to pack."

"Of course. I'm sorry. That must have been terrifying."

Behind them is the sound of a baby crying. A young girl calls out, "Beverly!"

"Eve! This is my family."

Eve holds the baby on her chest and pats her back. "Anah and Yemo, it's so nice to meet you! I've heard so much about you."

"Nice to meet you, Eve," I get closer to look at her baby. "What's her name?"

"Grace. It's my husband's mother's name," she says with some sadness.

"She beautiful." I point in the direction of where Amari works, handing out boxes of supplies and food to get everyone started. "That woman there, her name is Amari, she'll get you situated. Let me know if there's anything I can do."

"Thank you!" She says as she continues with the flow of people.

I look at Mom. "Her husband?"

Mom's eyes have that look when she's upset. "I'll tell you about it later."

"We have so much to talk about."

Sophia turns away to vomit. I run over to help and hold back her hair. "What's going on? Why are you both feeling sick?"

"Your bodies are adjusting," says Yemo.

Sophia throws up again. "Adjusting to what? And how long is this going to last?"

"Don't worry, it shouldn't last a couple of days." Yemo takes Sophia's hand. "The walk to the house will help."

If You Don't Leave, You'll Never Be Able to Come Back

A congregation gathers in the main field under the full moons, shining on the drummers. Bonfires grow in size and number. With joyous hearts, we dance and celebrate the success of the mission and sing songs of praise for their safe return. Paki and Amari sit by the fire and enjoy each other's embrace as they exchange stories with Yemo, Sophia, and Emily. Sophia has taken a liking to Eve and her baby girl, Grace. Mom and Meirlies dance together on the other side of the bonfire.

A breeze flows through the field and caresses our faces. The bonfires grow higher. Still feeling the effects of my quest, I move in a trance, like I did at the singing rocks, and go to that special place where body meets Spirit. Even in the worst of times, this place will bring me peace. Adversity can be confronted, maybe even embraced. It's hard to label this place or describe it with words, but if I had to give it a word, it would be freedom.

Missing the quiet of the wilderness, I wander to the trees to rest in the shadows. I look up at the stars and feel less alone. However, like a scratch I can't itch, a lingering dread haunts me. Everyone I love is here, except for one. He's stranded on a planet that's occupied by beings that wish to wield their power and evil will. They have lost but hopefully not the will to survive. By the time we arrive with another mission, it could be too late. I think about the battle they endured in the caldera on the hill. Guilt nags me. I should have been a part of the gang. In war, there's no time to soul search. You either have one or you don't.

My senses tell me I'm not alone. Behind me, someone or something watches. My heart beats faster. I recognize this sensation as "fight or flight". I felt it before on the station after the party on Thule. I'm in danger. I turn to run but trip and fall to the ground. Before the dark figure pounces on me, I spring back onto my feet. I'm without my scarf this evening. I realize this when I reach for it. I turn to fight my assailant. Sahn! He blocks my kick and flips me down on the ground. I roll back up and find myself running towards the flames of the bonfire. San reaches for me and grabs my shoulder. I run straight into the flames. I feel heat, and I'm surrounded by fire and smoke. I have no memory and feel completely disoriented. I look around for Yemo and my mother and father. Where did everyone go? I smell something repugnant, like burning flesh, or worse, dead Simerin. I move away from the fire and lean against a tree. There's a huge explosion, fifty yards away. I run towards the explosion and there's a view. I'm on top of a hill looking down to a landmass that's covered in snow. Dead bodies—Simerin bodies, lay in a sea of white. I finally recognize where I am. I did it again—jumped too far.

Moaning sounds come from a group of boulders. Someone is hurt. Cautiously, I walk around an outcrop of rocks and look down on a man wearing an eye patch. Emily told me about him, he saved their lives. He holds a grenade on his chest getting ready to kill us both.

"Stop!"

"Who's there?"

"You don't know me. Emily told me about you. I need to get back before it's too late, and you're coming with me."

"I'm not swimming to the chambers."

"You're not going to the chambers."

He climbs to his feet. His forehead bleeds, and he holds his dislocated shoulder. "I'm not leaving."

"If you don't leave, you'll never be able to come back."

"I wasn't planning to." He looks down at the turquoise necklace around my neck. "I know that necklace."

"Yes. Victor used to wear it. Emily gave it to me." I remove the necklace and hang it on a branch of a pinion tree.

"How..."

"I don't have time to explain!" I'm hyper-anxious and must force his willingness with mind tricks.

Approaching in droves are creatures moving with great speed, agility, and strength across the valley. These must be the Satans. They storm up the hill, getting ready to overtake us in seconds. Jumping back will be impossible. The rock outcrop makes up part of a cliff. I look over the edge. "Willy, we must go!" I grab Willy and force us off the cliff. Willy throws the grenade at the creatures jumping after us. The last thing I remember is the blast from the explosion.

Amahsah

I'm not breathing, and I'm unable to see. Muffled voices come from the darkness. I open my mouth to get air, but there's nothing. I'm holding onto something, and that something turns out to be someone. Those creatures jumped off the cliff after us without hesitation. I feel a hand pulling and tugging on my arm. I fight and scream. I'm breathing again, but I'm still unable to see. The voices speak another language. It sounds familiar. It's not Simerin or Monahdah. I'm still holding onto this body. The body isn't breathing. Someone pours water on him. Willy! He isn't breathing, and his heart has stopped. Someone beats on his chest and breathes into his mouth.

Someone drags me out of the mud pit where they make adobe bricks. A small crowd gathers outside their home. I try to understand what they say. I hear them discuss me; I disappeared, apparently, seven days ago. Yemo and Meirlies are beside me. They telepathically communicate with me. They want to take me home and in recovery as soon as possible. I don't argue. I'm too weak to argue. Meirlies lifts me and carries me away. I pass out into the darkness.

I awake to the sound of footsteps behind me. I jolt off the Mon table, on high alert, ready to defend myself.

"It's just me. Meirlies."

I'm dizzy and rest back down on the Mon table. I'm inside a large pyramid. The walls are adorned with Monahdah script and hand-carved relief sculptures depicting Monahdah's history, as well as prophetic futures. The queen, Nahanah, holds a large sunflower in one hand and a flaming torch in the other. Above her head are interlocking triangles, like Victor's tattoo. *"How long have I been in here?"*

"Three days. How do you feel?"

"A little dizzy."

"You'll do some good to go for a walk."

I inhale deeply. *"How's Willy?"*

"He suffered a heart attack, but he'll be fine."

When Meirlies says, 'Fine,' I'm triggered. "His home has been destroyed. People have been slaughtered. And Victor! You left him!"

"Anah. We waited. Everyone, including your mother, wouldn't be here. We would have lost everything."

"What about Sahn?"

"Yemo almost captured him."

I catch my breath. Talking feels arduous. *"I should have stayed at home fighting alongside Victor."*

"You're better off here."

"It doesn't feel like it. You want me here. You want me there. When do I get to decide?"

"Anah!" Mom says, breathless, entering the Mon chambers with Yemo. "Are you okay? I was so scared."

We hug. "I'm fine, Mom. Better than ever."

"I don't think you should do...well, whatever you did. It's not..."

"I know. I didn't try to do that. This traitor, Sahn, has been after me. He wants me gone."

"Yemo came between you and him, right before you ran into the fire," Meirlies says. "But he absconded once again."

Yemo's face reddens with frustration. I've seen that look before when he tried to beat the crap out of Victor.

AmanKi steps into the room. "We have scouts out to bring him in."

"AmanKi!" I give him a big embrace. I'm not sure if I should say congratulations on the success of the Chantallah mission or how sorry I am about Victor.

"You gave everyone a scare," he says. "I remember the first time I saw you jump, beating Victor in that race."

"I didn't know what I was doing then, and I don't know what I'm doing now."

"You just have to dial everything back." His voice is calm and reassuring, much like it was on that day he learned that I was Monahdah.

"Victor and those hiding in your underground chambers need rescuing as soon as possible. From what I saw, Earth is gone. These Satans are Simerin on steroids and are made for one thing—extermination."

AmanKi looks to Meirlies, and they nod. "What is it?" I ask.

AmanKi looks up at the carvings. "Something similar has happened before, also in a war with Simerin, not long before we terraformed NeuMonah."

"Where?"

"We colonized NinaKi, the planet you know as, Mars."

"What happened?" Mom says.

"According to historical accounts going back two hundred million years, after Simerin tried to occupy the colony, we destroyed the planet. We vowed never again and agreed to a treaty."

"The same treaty they broke again and again. Leading us to where we are today," says Yemo.

"You're right," says Meirlies. "The treaty is moot."

"Your solution is to destroy Earth? There must be a better, more rational solution."

AmanKi looks up at the wall, reflecting on Monahdah's past, beautifully recorded through the meticulously carved reliefs. "Their leader feels threatened by our growth and wants to destroy our civilizations."

"What civilizations?"

He points to the Mon table. "Mon regenerates Monahdah. It's in our DNA. That is what they want to destroy. Taking away our resources; Mon, NinaKi, civilizations, like the Vibans, and now Earth, will weaken us."

I shake my head. "This Simerin leader has a giant ego and an army to boot. Earth has been blocked, and we can't penetrate this barrier."

"Emily came to us while you were gone and told us that our mission failed," says AmanKi.

"Perhaps, the entire planet is not blocked," says Yemo. "There could be a way in."

"Victor is working on that," says Meirlies.

"Why didn't you say something?"

"He is getting ready for us."

"Victor's birth name is, Amahsah," says AmanKi. "It means defender. His mother named him this. It was too painful for him to carry because it was a constant reminder of her death. Now he lives up to his name, defending those who can't defend themselves, rescuing everyone he can. If it's the last thing I do, I will not leave him stranded." He looks at my mother. "Chantallah would not be here without him. It's not just a job to him but his life, driving him, and keeping him alive."

I rub my hand over my feather. "Every minute that we stand here is another wasted."

"Before you were attacked, we were developing a plan," Yemo says.

I look over at my mom. She cries. I notice that she holds something in her closed hand. "Mom, I know you feel responsible, but this is not your fault. Victor didn't start this war. Simerin did."

"I know. I'm scared of losing all of you." She opens her hand. "I found this in the field near the bonfire."

"My ring! Sahn must have dropped it." I slip it onto my finger remembering the first time I did, and it feels like a lifetime ago. "Thanks, Mom." I hug her, and I can feel how all of this is affecting her. "It's going to be okay." Simultaneously, I telepath to the others. *I would like to discuss this plan further.*

"We shall meet after sundown at Te-eha Aman," Meirlies says.

Yemo nods. *"I will summon Keepers."*

Te-eha Aman

Keepers gather around Meirlies in Peace Valley, Te-eha Aman. Faces glow and their long shadows stretch across the valley floor. A grand monolith towers above us, standing before a large pool of water that's a hundred yards long.

"Since we know that Victor is alive," Meirlies begins, "we hope he can dismantle the barrier, allowing us to enter through this corridor," he points in the darkness to a large holographic map of the region, "the four corner's region."

"What about what Emily said?" I say. "She said that our first attempt failed, and this is our first attempt."

Yemo shakes his head. "But Victor knows about the barrier now, and so do we. We didn't know this before. This could be another first attempt with new information."

"There isn't another first attempt. It's either our first or it's not."

"We can't get too hung up on that. What matters now is we know where to get through the barrier," says AmanKi. "Directly over the four corner's region. We must drop completely undetected. We can do that from the stratosphere or mesosphere. We'll pack three days of necessities, and the trek should take two and a half days."

"Hold on. What do you mean drop from the stratosphere?"

Yemo smiles. "He means, Anah, like a skydiver." He whistles and demonstrates with his hand falling from the sky.

"At 100,000 feet? That's space diving, not skydiving, and that's crazy." I shake my head. "The temperatures alone are negative 100."

"120," corrects Yemo. "And only 20% oxygen."

"I'm not going in like that."

"That's good, because you're not," says Meirlies. "You'll stay with Paki on the ship."

"What!" My voice echoes across the valley. "No way in hell will I stay back this time!"

"Anah, we'll discuss at another time."

Yemo laughs. "I warned you."

"I'm a Keeper. There's nothing more to discuss. I will be treated just like my brother, and everyone else."

"It's dangerous, and with Victor, you could make an emotional mistake," Meirlies says sourly.

"So could you." I look into the eyes of all the Keepers. "So could any of you."

AmanKi places his hand on my shoulder. "You're going. I wouldn't have it any other way."

Above us, Hopi villagers gather around a large fire. Their voices descend into the valley. An elder sings, and others join him. Men, women, and children gather around to listen. They sing under the cover of darkness to process the pain in their hearts and weep for the people they've lost, and the home they will never see again. Looking up to an unfamiliar sky, they praise God for the new home they've been granted, a new heaven on a new Earth. I feel their gratitude and recognize a similar grief in my heart, which is only a fraction of what they feel. I swallow the lump in my throat and tears spill over. "The question remains. What should we do about Earth?"

"We might have to destroy Ki to save it."

"We'll find Victor, first. I mean, that's the point of going back." My father nods. All the Keepers agree.

Willy stands on top of the hillside and watches the gathering of Keepers. They speak without words, but he understands. They study the hologram, and he recognizes his country. They are planning, and so is he.

Stowaway

Paki kisses the kids. "I love you, Oni. I love you, Davu. Take care of Mama." He turns to Amari. She hugs Paki and doesn't let go.

"Please, Paki. Not this time."

"I wouldn't be able to live with myself if I stay behind."

"It doesn't feel right. I have a bad feeling."

"You've said that before. But I come back. I always do. This mission is much bigger than us. I'm doing it for the sake of the future...your future, the kids."

Amari looks at her husband, she thinks, for the last time. Paki kisses her and walks into the pod.

I'm not ready to turn around and see my mother's worried face. This time, at least, I'm able to say goodbye. The circumstances are different. I'm not running away or retreating. It's on my terms. I'm fighting, rescuing, liberating. I trained for this, and I'm ready. Finally, I turn to face them. I stand tall and proud so that they might also. When I look into their eyes, I feel their fear, and my knees tremble. Sophia kisses Yemo goodbye. She blows me a kiss and then puts her arm around Mom. I run off the platform and hug Mom one last time.

"I love you, Anah," she says.

I hold her tightly. "I'm not coming back until we get Victor, but I'm coming back."

Sophia hugs Yemo. "Don't come back until you kick some Simerin ass."

We board the pod and wave goodbye. The hatch door closes. I look at Yemo. "That was probably the hardest part of this mission."

"I hope." He taps my shoulder. "Come. We have work to do."

Most of the crew members work on the ship and its day-to-day functions. Keepers prepare for battle and the rescue mission. I try to keep a lower profile and blend in with the others. Meirlies could change his mind at any moment. I don't know if he could prevent me from going, but I know he will try. I wish he would accept the fact that I'm capable of making my own decisions.

We report to Yemo, our captain, every twenty hours, which is now. He gives us our tasks. "Now you will choose your Kisnah Dahman." He looks at me. "Your buddy and guardian. You and your Kisnah will train together. Never leave your Kisnah and always work together, seamlessly. Spar together, not against, but with. Run together, eat together, think together, everything together." I glance around the room and try to make eye contact. I walk over to a Keeper, but he turns to join another Keeper. I try again and again. I stand alone and embarrassed.

"Anah, it's okay," Yemo sighs. "They're just scared."

A Keeper steps forward. "ShanahMi, Anah. Your father will kill us if we...if something should happen."

Another Keeper named, Tun, walks up to me, bows, and says, "Lamu Nahma, KisnahMi."

I bow feeling grateful for his courage. "Lamu Nahma, Tun. KisnahMi."

"Anah, Meirlies wants to see you," says Yemo.

"Why doesn't he just ask me?"

"Right away," Meirlies says. "Both of you."

"Okay. On our way."

The door to the main bridge opens as Tun, Yemo, and I enter.

"Why does Tun come with you?" Meirlies asks.

"He's my Kisnah."

"I see. We will discuss this later."

"There's nothing to discuss."

"I'm starting to really like her," says a voice from behind.

"Willy? What on Earth are you doing here?"

"Earth?" With his one eye and his new eyepatch, he looks through the large window that frames only darkness. Every strand of his hair has turned silver after our jump. "Not sure where that is. Hopefully, that's where we're going."

"I don't think it's where you want to be," I say.

"We have a stowaway," Meirlies huffs.

"We will decide what is best." Everyone turns to look at Tun. He took the words right out of my mouth. I think I like this buddy concept. Meirlies furrows his brow.

I feel Tun's heart beating fast. "Willy can come with us, I mean, and we will work it out." There's a long pause. Meirlies agrees, and we turn to leave.

"Wait, Anah." I turn to face my father. Tun stands next to me. "Just Anah," he says to Tun.

Tun doesn't move. "Anah is my Kisnah."

"Okay. I'll go along with this, for now." He stares directly into my eyes. He thinks of my mother. He promised her that no harm would come to me. His eyes well with tears. "Emily." He swallows hard. "She told me the mission returns successfully, however..."

"However what?"

"However, Victor does not return with us."

"I don't understand."

"If you don't go, then, maybe..."

"That's a bunch of bull! What if I don't go? The mission isn't successful but then Victor returns?"

"She didn't know, exactly. She didn't want you to know."

"She's right about that. You shouldn't have told me. The mission is Victor!"

I leave the bridge, brush past Willy, and march to my quarters. Tun sits while I pace from one end to the other.

"Unbelievable! Why did he tell me this? This is such bullshit! He doesn't want me to go. That's all!"

"You wished he kept this information to himself?"

"This isn't information. This is Emily and her visions."

Willy stands outside the semi-transparent door, and I let him in. "Oh, Willy! I'm sorry. Please, come in. Do you have everything you need?"

"Yes. Yemo gave me his room across from you. Can I speak to you about what your father said?"

"I'm sorry you had to hear that. What do you want to tell me?"

"I don't know about this vision...what Emily saw or didn't. But I do know that things unfold as they happen, so, don't let what he told you influence your decision."

"I mean, how could it not?"

"Victor said to us, once, after the horses carried us through snow drifts waist high, and over a hundred Simerin tracking us. We argued amongst ourselves and took it out on Emily. Victor heard us argue, and this angered him. It was the only time I saw him get angry. He said our future isn't written in stone. What happens, happens, and that's all there is to it."

Hearing Willy quote Victor helps calm me, and I collect myself. "Thank you for sharing this, Willy. You are right. I'm sorry for what you've been through. I'm glad that you're okay, and that you're here with us. Please let me know if you need anything."

The door slides open as he turns to leave. "Only one thing...get me back home."

I want to promise Willy that we will, but I can't. I look deep into his eyes. They are older, yet wiser and somehow clearer. "We'll do everything we can, but...what will you do there? There's nothing left."

"Uglies. As long as I'm still breathing, I'll fight. No one should be able to invade and have complete disregard for life. No one."

Willy's words ring true. As we train for the next 12 and a half months, I keep them in mind. As long as I still breathe, I'll fight. Whatever happens, happens. However first, we must save Victor.

The End of Part 2

Vocabulary

Mon - Rock/planet. A special stone from planet Mon that has cosmic energy.

Monahdah - An all-male race from planet Mon.

Simerin - Enemy alien race of the Monahdah.

NeuMonah - New Planet colonized by the Monahdah.

Chantallah - The chosen

Anah - Sister/female brother

Mahna - Brother

Meirlies - Father

Minniedah - My son

Nahanah - Goddess

Adamah- Human

Drohan - Traitor

Nahmah - I love you/Greetings

PrimmonKi - Female from Earth

Lamu Nahma - Thank you/I graciously accept

MiLamu Nahma - You're welcome/I graciously give

Ki - Earth

AmanKi - Peace, and the name of Victor's father.

Dahman - Guardian

DahmanKi - Guardian of peace

Vunsch - Wonderful/Congratulations

Elohim Davunsch - The celebration was wonderful.

Da - Is/was/here

MinnEnKi - Earth Lord. Name of Anah's father

ShanahMi - Forgive me

Nos - We shall

SzusahDah - Unite

Ma - And

Florah - Proser/flourish/bloom

ShanahMi - I'm sorry

AhnehMi - I accept/I take

Kisnah - Shadow

Tulah - Source/God power

Ziel - Intention

Zi - Heart